Julie Wassmer is a professional television drama writer who has worked on various series including ITV's *London's Burning*, C5's *Family Affairs* and BBC's *EastEnders* – on which she wrote for almost twenty years.

Her autobiography, *More Than Just Coincidence*, was Mumsnet Book of the Year 2011.

Find details of author events and other information about the Whitstable Pearl Mysteries at:
www.juliewassmer.com

T0363783

Also by Julie Wassmer

The Whitstable Pearl Mystery
Murder-on-Sea
May Day Murder
Murder on the Pilgrims Way
Disappearance at Oare
Murder Fest
Murder on the Downs
Strictly Murder
Murder at Mount Ephraim

JULIE WASSMER

MURDER at the ALLOTMENT

CONSTABLE

CONSTABLE

First published in Great Britain in 2024 by Constable

A CIP catalogue record for this book is
available from the British Library.

ISBN: 978-1-40871-994-7

Typeset in Adobe Caslon Pro by SX Composing DTP, Rayleigh, Essex
Printed and bound in Great Britain by Clays Ltd, Elcograf S.p.A.

Papers used by Constable are from well-managed forests
and other responsible sources.

Constable
An imprint of
Little, Brown Book Group
Carmelite House
50 Victoria Embankment
London EC4Y 0DZ

An Hachette UK Company
www.hachette.co.uk

www.littlebrown.co.uk

For all those taking care of
Whitstable's Stream Walk Community Garden

'A society grows great when old men plant trees whose shade they know they shall never sit in.'

Greek proverb

...every ground... by place...
... shall give...

CHAPTER ONE

If anyone had been up that Saturday morning, shortly before nine a.m., taking a walk near Prospect Field in Whitstable, they might well have assumed that the tall, dark-haired woman wearing a vintage summer dress, who was approaching from her parked Fiat with a pannier across her shoulder, might have been heading to some public benches that overlooked the shore. Perched high on the railway embankment, they afforded a fine view of the Swale estuary, while providing a suitable resting place for any dog walkers who preferred to avoid the beach and the crowds who flocked to it during the summer months.

Prospect Field was the name given to an area of almost four acres of scrub and grassland between Whitstable's railway line on the north side and the residential road of Joy Lane to the south. Preserved by a group of volunteers, it offered a much-needed safe habitat for local flora and fauna, especially as a proliferation of new building projects had left few wildlife corridors in the area – apart from the golf course and the railway embankment. It was a peaceful spot, not just for local walkers but for a variety of creatures, including hedgehogs, woodpeckers, grass snakes and lizards – as well as the rabbits that were often seen scampering down the embankment.

As the bells of St Alfred's Church began to ring the hour, Pearl Nolan was quickly reminded that she had little time before another busy day would begin for her at the restaurant that bore her name – The Whitstable Pearl. The popular high-street establishment had supported Pearl and her family for the past twenty years, and as a 'people person', she always did her best to ensure her customers enjoyed their time with her, locals and visitors alike. At one time, The Whitstable Pearl had presented a huge challenge for a young single mother with only the support of her mother, Dolly, but now, some twenty years on and in her early forties, Pearl found the business ticked over nicely with the help of a talented young chef and a few trusted members of staff.

Taking a deep breath and a set of keys from her pocket, Pearl quickly crossed a path that led to a local allotment site where a rusting gate creaked open beneath her hand, signalling that someone else was already there. The ground was still damp from a heavy downpour the night before, but as Pearl gazed up at the sky, she could see the sun trying to break through the morning haze.

The Nolan allotment had been passed down through generations of Pearl's family to her mother, though it was

Pearl who generally tended the produce grown there, with some help from her son, Charlie. Dolly preferred to potter in the plot's wooden cabin, particularly when she had some messy artwork to complete. Her usual signature pieces were small canvases inspired by the local coastline and embellished with various *objets trouvés* she picked up on her beachcombing walks: dried seaweed, shells and fragments of glass polished by the tide until they resembled jewels.

As Dolly had long surrendered most of her own garden to a new extension that enabled her to accommodate holiday guests in the first-floor flat she had named Dolly's Attic, the allotment provided some welcome open space, as it did also for Pearl: her garden at Seaspray Cottage, though attractive and with a sea-facing view, had shrunk with the inclusion of a beach hut on her lawn, which she now used as an office. The allotment also offered Pearl a valuable location on which she could grow not only her own fruit and vegetables but flowers too – like the seemingly unending supply of sweet peas she used throughout the summer to decorate her restaurant tables.

Although a few neighbouring plots had changed hands after their holders had given up on them, shocked by the hard work that was required – as opposed to the idealised allotment life displayed in TV shows and colour supplements – Pearl had held on to the Nolan plot. She respected her family roots and appreciated a wider sense of history: she had read of how early allotments had grown out of the theft, for want of a better word, of common land that had been lost to the enclosures. At school, Pearl had learned that the concept of allotting to poor labourers a piece of land on which they could grow their own food had evolved during the Enlightenment. Then the ruling classes had deemed it safer for peasants to be planting root crops than pursuing more wayward habits.

Once the Industrial Revolution had forced people off the land into mills and factories, it became clear that a large proportion of the population could no longer feed itself; the allocation of 'allotments' of land represented some insurance against starvation. Following the First World War, this provision had been extended to returning soldiers, with local authorities providing land according to demand. As Dolly's grandmother had always said, 'As long as you have a piece of land to put a spade into, you'll never go hungry.'

Pearl had no fear of starvation, merely a firm intention to make good use of the plot while taking time to relax from the demands of The Whitstable Pearl. These days, her presence wasn't always needed in the restaurant as her small group of capable staff could manage quite well without her. But no matter how busy Pearl became, she always found time for some allotment planting in spring, even though the resulting crops were not always a success. What was important to her, as with her cooking, was to experiment and discover new ways of achieving good results. The allotment also allowed her to feel connected to the earth. By turning it, feeding it and making use of it in a positive way, stillness seemed to fall, as though the earth itself was giving thanks.

In spite of the peaceful environment, in recent months the allotments had become the setting for a battle with the local council, which had not only sold off half of the site but voted to reduce the size of existing plots. Considerable strips had been lost from each to create more council revenue while satisfying increasing demands from an influx of newcomers – the DFLs, or Down From Londoners, as local people tended to describe them. The term had become increasingly pejorative, particularly since one new resident, in particular, had succeeded in pressuring the local newspaper, the *Chronicle*, to feature her views in several front-page stories. She had claimed it was easier to find a burial plot in Whitstable than a space on a local allotment – a point she had later pressed home in a powerful speech at a rowdy council meeting.

It was no secret that Caroline Lanzi was particularly well versed in the art of public relations. In fact, it was widely known that she owned a successful London-based company, Lanzi Communications, which specialised in generating good publicity for clients – including some minor celebrities. Once the new DFL had bought a house in Whitstable's Joy Lane, close to the allotments, it had soon become clear that she was using her professional skills to obtain exactly what she wanted – even if other plot holders, like Pearl and Dolly, were to lose out on allotment territory.

Pearl glanced across the site, relieved that neither Caroline Lanzi nor her husband, Franco, was anywhere to be seen. In fact, no one appeared to be working on the plots, in spite of the unlocked gate. The neighbouring allotment to Pearl's belonged to Marty Smith, owner of Cornucopia, the local fruit and vegetable shop – or, rather, emporium, as Marty preferred to call it. At that hour, he would still be supervising deliveries for his best customers – including Pearl at the restaurant – before enjoying a busy day providing exotic fruit smoothies for tourists and fresh produce for locals.

Marty's plot sat beside that of local wood carver Joe Fuller and his partner, Florence Brightling. A gentle nonconformist couple in their early thirties, their plot was filled with an abundance of well-tended runner beans, strawberries, tomato plants and squash of various colours, shapes and sizes.

The next belonged to local teacher Michael Stopes. In recent weeks, Pearl had noticed how well Michael had seemed to be getting on with his own plot neighbour, Vanessa Hobbs, a teaching assistant at the local nursery who kept three hens on her patch, named Faith, Hope and Charity. Across the fence from a coop that kept the birds safe from marauding foxes lay a plot acquired by Caroline Lanzi's friends, Victor and Natasha Bessant – owners of two shops in Harbour Street, which had recently been renovated to create a spacious new art gallery – The Front. Dolly maintained that the name was entirely appropriate not only due to the gallery's enormous show window but the high rates of commission she claimed were shamefully charged for sales of work created by impoverished local artists.

Dolly's old friend Madge Tolliday had custody of the next plot, while Caroline and Franco Lanzi held land on the other side. Bordering the Lanzis' plot, Ted Rowden, an octogenarian, was the local expert on all things horticultural. It was perfectly possible, thought Pearl, that beyond the cloches, cold frames and bamboo wigwams, the grandfather of Joy Lane's allotments might be ensconced in his shed, busily sowing seeds or perhaps enjoying a flask of tea to fuel him for a morning's weeding. There again, thought Pearl, he might also be contemplating how to deal with the bindweed that was fast encroaching across the fence of the final plot, from which Ted's neighbour, David Chappell, had been noticeably absent for some considerable time.

As far as Pearl was aware, no one on the allotments had tackled David about the state of his plot, because it was common knowledge he had been experiencing problems. Everyone seemed to know that his wife, Cindy, had left him for local roofer and scaffolder Russ Parker, nicknamed Russell the Muscle due to his highly toned physique. Russ Parker's bronzed 'abs' seemed always on display on the rooftops of Whitstable – which Pearl knew would have added to David's distress. Although his wife and her lover had recently left town, David had seemingly descended into an even greater downward spiral, convincing Pearl that he must have been holding on to some hope that Cindy might tire of a T-shirt full of muscles and return to him.

Dolly had heard, through her own local jungle telegraph, that David had suffered a breakdown but had chosen to ignore suggestions to seek help from his GP. Thinking about this now, Pearl considered the bindweed spreading out from David's plot and realised that, with all that he had had to deal with lately, the allotment must surely have been the last thing on his mind. No one expected David Chappell to return to it until he recovered.

In contrast, Pearl's family plot remained well tended and easily identified by the large decorative panel that was attached to the side of its cabin. All Dolly's work, it featured an oyster and a totem pole with a burnished sun shining down on a burgeoning crop. A snazzily dressed scarecrow, wearing an old striped blazer and a Panama hat, stood guard among beds of colourful sweet peas and summer vegetables. Pearl smiled at her crop and quickly hurried across to the cabin, outside which marguerites in terracotta pots swayed in the breeze as if greeting her arrival.

Pearl searched for the cabin's key in her pannier, then slipped it into the lock and entered. As she pushed back a pair of striped curtains at the window, daylight filled the dusty interior, falling upon a small French wood-burning stove with an art-nouveau motif on its grille. Dolly had bought it from a junk shop long ago and it had often been put to good use in the winter months, though it would remain redundant today.

Taking a flask from her bag, Pearl reached for an enamel mug from a kitchen cabinet that had somehow survived the Blitz and poured herself some strong tea. Scooping up her long dark hair she secured it with a comb from her pocket before taking her phone from her bag and dialling a number.

The reply came quickly. 'Pearl?'

'How are you feeling today?' she asked, as she sat down in a rocking chair.

At the other end of the line, DCI Mike McGuire stared ruefully down at his left leg, the lower part of which was encased in blue plaster. 'Hot,' he replied tersely.

'Well,' Pearl began, 'that's a given if you're having to wear a cast at this time of year. Hopefully you'll feel more comfortable after your check-up today.'

'They're not taking it off, Pearl,' McGuire explained, 'just checking the angle of my foot.'

There was no mistaking the frustration in his tone. Lately there seemed no placating McGuire, which was unsurprising as his severed Achilles tendon was preventing him from doing all the things he enjoyed most – including his work at Canterbury CID.

'How about I come to the hospital with you?' suggested Pearl.

'You've got too much to do. And I don't want you to waste your day.'

'It won't be wasted,' Pearl argued. 'I'll be with you.' She paused. Then: 'It's the least I can do if you won't let me take proper care of you.'

McGuire heaved a troubled sigh. 'I told you,' he began, 'I'm a bad patient, Pearl, and I don't want "looking after".'

She ventured: 'In sickness and in health?'

'We're not married.'

'Yet,' said Pearl, quickly, 'but we could be.'

'We *will* be,' said McGuire, 'but I'm not hobbling down an aisle any time soon.'

He pulled down his trouser leg to cover the wretched cast. He hadn't acquired the injury while pursuing a dangerous criminal but instead during an innocuous game of squash – about which his colleagues on the force had continued to rib him.

'Heard anything from Charlie?' he asked, in an effort to change the subject. Pearl's son had disappeared to spend time with a Welsh girlfriend on the Gower Peninsula.

'We FaceTimed the other night,' said Pearl. 'He'd just been surfing on Rhossili Beach. It looked heavenly, and Cerys is very pretty too – his new girlfriend.'

'Lucky Charlie,' said McGuire, pleased for him.

'Let me drive you to your appointment,' said Pearl, unwilling to be distracted.

'I've already ordered a cab. Pearl, I'm fine.'

'You're not. You're a cranky invalid.'

'You're right,' said McGuire, giving up. 'Just keep reminding me of that.'

With that, he grabbed the crutches that had been loaned to him by the physio department at the local hospital and caught sight of himself in his wardrobe mirror. 'Long John Silver had nothing on me.'

'Apart from a parrot,' said Pearl.

A car's horn sounded sharply from the street outside and McGuire glanced from his window to see a cab waiting patiently outside. 'I've got to go.'

'Wait!' Pearl organised her thoughts, knowing she had little time to tell him how sorry she was that this accident, and his attitude towards it, should be keeping them apart. Instead she said only: 'Tell them to take good care of you or . . .'

'Or?'

'They'll have me to deal with.'

McGuire finally allowed himself to smile then ended the call.

Now Pearl took a deep breath. She felt conflicted, relieved that McGuire's injury hadn't sabotaged any existing wedding plans, but confident she didn't need a marriage certificate to prove what she felt for him. Things weren't straightforward. Coming from a man who was so married to his work, McGuire's proposal had been a complete surprise – perhaps so much so that she had accepted it without fully acknowledging what marriage to the detective might actually mean: the relinquishing of her independence, and perhaps even her job – not at the restaurant but the side hustle through which she had first met McGuire, in her role as a local private investigator.

After she'd started up Nolan's Detective Agency, it had never occurred to Pearl that her work might extend beyond the cases she felt more than adequately equipped to solve: tracing missing persons and pets, stalking errant spouses and recovering stolen vehicles – missions entrusted to her by members of her own close-knit community. What she hadn't counted on was that the agency would bring her into contact with McGuire – and murder.

That had prompted her to call upon the police training she had chosen to abandon more than twenty years ago on discovering herself to be pregnant with Charlie. Pearl had ended a potential career with the police, only to find herself returning to a life of crime – this time outside the force. A series of events had thrust her together with McGuire, convincing her that she was back on the path for which she had always felt destined. Somehow, like the 'volunteer' hollyhocks that had appeared along the inhospitable stony path leading to the allotment, Pearl had found the setting in which she not only belonged but could thrive.

With that in mind, she now set about achieving what she had come to the allotment to do: to check on the condition of a crop of purslane, the leafy, frost-tender plant she loved to use as a herb and a salad vegetable. Today she would toss it into a simmering pot of clams to ensure some lemony accents in the dish she planned to prepare. Its tangy taste was always strongest when harvested early in the day so she finished her tea and screwed the top back on to her flask. She was about to move outside when she was halted by several loud bangs beyond the cabin – followed by a desperate cry.

Rushing outside, Pearl stared across the plots to see a figure facing away from her, holding a rake high in the air, then bringing it down hard upon a cold frame. The shocking clatter of shattered glass pierced the peaceful morning. A flock of birds took to the sky. A dog began barking nearby. She cried: 'David? Is that you?'

As the figure turned towards her, Pearl saw that she was right. David Chappell stared back at her, looking lost until he gazed distractedly at the rake clutched in his hand then hurled it across the allotment. He buried his face in his hands and sank slowly to his knees as though all strength had deserted him.

Pearl rushed across the site and found him crouching among chaos, his once orderly plot now overgrown to the point that there was no visible path or any sense of where borders began or ended. 'What on earth's happened?' she asked.

At this, David's hands slid from his face and he surveyed the destruction surrounding him, the smashed cold frame and shattered glass embedded in tall weeds. He looked up, dazed, prompting Pearl to help him to his feet. 'Why would you do this?' she asked. 'Aren't you here to look after your plot?'

David Chappell shook his head slowly. 'It isn't mine,' he said dully, 'not any more.'

Confused, Pearl eyed him, watching his hand move slowly to his pocket from which he pulled out a folded letter. 'This came today,' he murmured, handing it to her. 'In the post.'

Pearl began reading. She frowned, puzzled by the contents. 'I don't understand.'

'Neither did I,' said David, 'at first. But it's really quite simple . . . They're taking this away from me. Look.' He grabbed the letter from her hand. 'It states quite clearly that this is an under-cultivation notice. I haven't planted enough to satisfy the council.'

Pearl re-read some of the letter. 'It also says that the council contacted you twenty-eight days ago with a warning about this.'

David remained silent.

'Well?' asked Pearl, gently. 'Did you receive a warning?'

Her allotment neighbour shook his head again. 'I . . . don't know,' he admitted. 'I can't remember.' He stared back at her, helplessly. 'It was a bad time. I let the post pile up. I don't remember seeing anything from the council.'

'Perhaps you forgot?' asked Pearl, tentatively.

David seemingly held on to this thought like a drowning man to a life raft. 'Yes,' he said, rubbing his brow. 'I've had a lot on my mind.'

'Of course,' said Pearl, her tone now encouraging him to explain further.

'I couldn't have come here then,' he went on. 'I couldn't cope. With anything.'

Pearl nodded. 'I know,' she said calmly, 'but things are better now.'

'*Are* they?' he said brusquely. 'How?' His raised voice caused her to flinch but he continued nonetheless. 'They're taking this away from me!'

'I'm sure we can do something,' said Pearl, trying to remain in control. 'If we go to the council and explain—'

'Explain what? That I've been driven half mad by what happened with Cindy and—' He broke off, his face crumpling.

'I'll help,' said Pearl. 'We'll get this sorted.'

'We can't,' said David. 'It's too late, don't you see?' He stared at her. 'They're acting on a complaint. They don't want me here.' He took on a hunted look.

'Who are you talking about?' asked Pearl, warily.

'Who do you think?' David waved towards the other plots, his gaze focusing on one in particular, with a timber deck, two stylish loungers and a neat path dividing flowers from vegetables, all in stark contrast to the disorder of David's.

'Caroline?' said Pearl.

David looked back at her. 'Who else?' he said coldly. 'I can't really blame her. Why would she want a madman like me so close by?'

Pearl reflected on this, recognising that Caroline Lanzi's plot was sheer perfection, a colour supplement dream, beside the chaos of David's, which clearly reflected the disturbance of his mind. Pearl found herself unable to offer a suitable answer as she began to comprehend the extent of David Chappell's distress. The disintegration of his marriage and the loss of the woman he loved to another man had transformed him from the quiet neighbour he had always been to the disturbed individual now standing before her, capable of such violence on his own neglected territory.

He was still staring at Pearl, waiting for an answer, when the moment was broken by the sound of Pearl's mobile. She answered the call to hear her mother's voice. 'Whatever you're doing,' Dolly began, 'leave it. You need to get to the restaurant, Pearl. Now.' The line went dead in Pearl's hand.

CHAPTER TWO

Half an hour later, Pearl was ensconced in The Whitstable Pearl, which had not yet opened for the day. Several people were with her at a table, including Dolly, whose seascape paintings adorned the restaurant walls. Pearl's young waitress, Ruby, was serving mugs of tea and biscuits to the assembled guests while Pearl was studying a number of letters spread out on the table, all bearing the council's insignia of a prancing white horse, a heraldic image known as Invicta, or the White Horse of Kent.

'Now let me get this straight,' Pearl began. 'We've *all* received letters from the council?'

'That's right,' Dolly confirmed. 'Someone's been busy lodging complaints, left, right and centre.'

A murmur of disgruntled agreement travelled around the table.

'But who?' said Pearl. 'And why?'

'Isn't it obvious?' said Dolly, ruefully.

'Your mum's right,' said Dolly's old friend Madge Tolliday. 'There's only one person with enough nerve to do something like this.'

David Chappell spoke up: 'I told you, Pearl. Caroline Lanzi!'

'It couldn't be anyone else,' said Michael Stopes. 'The woman's an absolute nightmare.'

Beside him, his allotment neighbour, Vanessa Hobbs, gave a quick nod but before she had a chance to speak, a voice sounded behind them. 'Well, I happen to think Mrs Lanzi is a very nice lady.'

Pearl's greengrocer, Marty Smith, was sauntering over from the direction of the kitchen, dressed in his signature green Cornucopia T-shirt, which matched the colour of his eyes. 'I've had plenty of dealings with Mr and Mrs Lanzi,' he added, 'and I've always found them to be very cultured and polite.'

Dolly eyed him. 'Customers of yours, Marty?'

He shrugged. 'What if they are?'

'Your views are partial,' Dolly warned him.

Marty went to protest but Pearl interceded. 'He's still entitled to them.'

'Thank you, Pearl,' he said.

'Even though we disagree with them,' she added.

Deflated, Marty offered her the piece of paper in his hand. Pearl put on her glasses to read it while Ted Rowden took off his own and leaned in to Marty to ask: 'You've had a letter too, have you?'

'As a matter of fact, I haven't,' Marty replied proudly. 'But then *I*'ve done nothing wrong.'

Pearl waved the piece of paper Marty had just given her and explained to Ted: 'This is only a receipt for a delivery Marty's just made.' She signed it and handed it back to Marty, who, though paying good money to three efficient delivery boys, always insisted on making Pearl's deliveries personally.

Pearl's greengrocer owned a large house in the neighbouring village of Tankerton and drove a convertible sports car that turned heads when it sped along the high street. By most people's standards, Marty Smith was an eligible bachelor although love had always eluded him. Girlfriends had come and gone, but no relationship had ever blossomed. After one date with him, long ago, Pearl had recognised why. During what was to have been a romantic meal in an expensive coastal restaurant in Broadstairs, Marty had explained to Pearl that he had always felt her to be a kindred spirit, someone who had earned his respect for the passionate way in which she ran her business. Then he proceeded to share his vision of a happy and fulfilled future in terms of cash flow and collateral, revenue and rates of return, balance sheets and bridging loans, and debating whether his plans for diversification would bring dividends or debt. That evening, over a candle-lit dinner, Pearl had recognised once and for all that Marty Smith would never light her fire, and if Marty knew it too, he had nevertheless clung to the hope of changing her mind – until Mike McGuire had entered her life. Nevertheless, Pearl couldn't help feeling that Marty would continue to wait in the wings, carefully observing whether or not her engagement to McGuire would ever result in marriage.

Madge leaned across the table to nudge Pearl. 'We had none of this, you know, before the Lanzis came on that allotment.'

Pearl handed back Marty's signed receipt, which he pocketed before commenting to Madge: 'Now now. Everyone's innocent until proved guilty.'

Madge continued: 'DFLs coming here—'

'Look who's talking!' said Marty, swiftly. 'You're hardly a Whitstable native, Madge. You're from London yourself!'

'Stepney,' said Madge, proudly. 'But my family had been coming to Kent for generations to pick hops, not to cause trouble for the locals with the council.'

Suitably stung, Marty sucked his teeth and headed back to the kitchen. Once he had left, Dolly piped up. 'Madge is right,' she said. 'I'll go and talk to Ratty.'

She began to get to her feet but Pearl stopped her. 'If anyone's going to talk to Councillor Radcliffe, it'll be me,' she said, 'but I need more information first.' She paused to gather her thoughts, then said: 'Let's go through this again.' She turned to Ted. 'Your bees are the subject of one complaint?'

Ted nodded. 'That's right, but I've kept bees on that lottie for decades. I've got written permission from the council and public liability insurance *and* I'm a member of the Bee Keepers Association. I've never once had any complaints and I've got a perfect right to keep 'em.'

'Well said, Ted,' commented Dolly, 'same as Vanessa here with her hens.'

Clearly trying to hide her distress, Vanessa Hobbs spoke up. 'You know my girls,' she began, in a trembling voice, 'they do no harm to anyone. I take good care of them. I'm at the allotment almost every day, sometimes before and after nursery. And they have a very safe fox-proof run. They're just happy to be alive,' she went on. 'I rescued them from a battery farm.'

'I know,' said Pearl. 'That was very kind of you – and their eggs are delicious,' she added. 'Thanks for letting me have some.'

'You're welcome.' Vanessa smiled so sweetly that in that moment she looked to Pearl more like a shy teen-ager than a thirty-something teaching assistant. The impression was reinforced by Michael Stopes patting her hand and offering a warm smile, as if to show how proud he was of her.

'And, Michael,' said Pearl, waiting until he looked back at her before she went on, 'it seems your wind chimes are a problem.'

'Not to me or anyone else I know,' he said. 'They've been up for over a year since I brought them back from my trip to China, so whoever's complained to the council . . .' He trailed off. 'They *must* be a newcomer.' Again, a nod of agreement circulated the table.

'Madge?' asked Pearl.

Madge Tolliday finished her tea and set her mug down smartly, pushing her mop of curly grey hair back behind her ears, exposing the pretty enamel earrings she was wearing in the shape of two swallows. 'Someone's decided my grass is too high,' she announced. 'They must have been round with a tape measure. Have they not heard of "no mow May"?'

Ted nudged her. 'It's July, Madge.'

'So I'm a bit late! And my pond's a health hazard apparently,' she added. 'Mosquitoes.' She tutted in disapproval. 'Hardly the Everglades, is it?'

Pearl now turned her attention to the two people who had remained quiet throughout. 'Joe and Florence?'

Joe Fuller shared a look with his partner, then admitted: 'Flo and I are in trouble, Pearl.'

'That's right,' said Florence, with a pained expression, as she flicked her long fair hair over one shoulder. 'Apart from growing our own veg, Joe's been using our allotment shed as a . . .'

She was unable to continue and Joe took up the thread. 'If you must know, I've been using it as a studio.'

Dolly frowned. 'What's so wrong with that?'

Florence looked perplexed. 'We've moved most of Joe's tools there – for his carvings – though the rest are now at home.'

Joe raked his hand through his long dark hair and seemed to brace himself. 'Someone's gone and complained that I'm using our shed for—'

'Creating something beautiful?' Dolly smiled, and gave a shrug. 'I've seen your work, Joe. You're a very talented young man.' She beamed in encouragement. 'And I wouldn't worry if I was you. I do some painting in our cabin from time to time, don't I, Pearl?'

Joe and Florence shared a look, which Pearl immediately understood. 'It's not quite the same, Mum.'

'Why?' asked Dolly, mystified.

'Because you're not exactly . . . a professional artist.'

Dolly frowned while Joe explained, 'I think what Pearl's trying to say, Dolly, is that if I'm using our allotment shed as my place of work, it's actually a business premises, so there may be implications about paying business rates.'

He stared down guiltily while Florence laid her hand on his and gave it a comforting squeeze, as she said: 'Joe lost his workshop recently through no fault of his own but . . . Well, the landlord put up the rent and . . .' She looked again at Joe beside her.

'I had some commissions,' Joe explained. 'I didn't want to let my clients down. To be honest, we couldn't really afford to.'

Dolly's frown deepened.

Florence added: 'We'd been hoping that Mr Bessant might take a piece of Joe's to sell. His wife, Natasha, told him she'd seen some of Joe's work.'

'At the allotment?' asked Pearl.

Joe nodded slowly. 'It was a Sunday afternoon, shortly after we'd lost the workshop, and I happened to be moving some pieces into the shed. They weren't finished but Natasha said how much she liked them and that she'd have a word with Victor for me.'

Dolly and Pearl caught each other's eye.

Florence spoke quickly. 'No. I know what you might be thinking but Caroline definitely wasn't there to see that.'

'But,' said Dolly, 'she and Natasha Bessant are as thick as thieves. And when it comes to that gallery doing favours for anyone, they might as well be stealing work from local creatives rather than exhibiting it. Seventy-five per cent commission?'

Joe looked away. 'Beggars can't be choosers, Dolly.'

'Philistines!' Dolly exclaimed. 'Those people know the price of everything and the value of nothing.' Picking up her own letter, she waved it around. 'And now the council has the gall to order me to take down my mural. Graffiti, they call it. The nerve! I'll do no such thing!'

'That's the spirit,' said Madge, turning to Ted beside her. 'And don't you go getting rid of your bees. If they want to start a fight with any one of us, they'll have to fight us all.'

'Maybe not *all* of us,' said Pearl, cautiously. 'You're forgetting that Marty hasn't received a letter.'

'Yes,' said Dolly, 'and that's probably because he's been sucking up to the Lanzis for custom.'

'And what about Natasha and Victor?' asked Florence. 'As you say, they're good friends with Caroline.'

Dolly nodded. 'Yes. So they've probably dodged a bullet too.'

David Chappell stared at his own letter. 'And meanwhile *I've* got an under-cultivation notice,' he said darkly.

'Don't you worry,' said Dolly. 'They can't threaten us all like this. Not if we stick together. We'll fight them on the beeches – *and* the oaks!'

A laugh went around at Dolly's pun, everyone apparently heartened by the idea of mounting a unified front – until a strange sound filled the room. Several mobile phones signalled in unison the arrival of a text. Everyone checked their messages. It was the same text on each phone:

> I've called an urgent meeting of all allotment holders this evening.
>
> Please be at my home in Joy Lane at 7 p.m. prompt.
>
> Caroline Lanzi

CHAPTER THREE

Mike McGuire had spent the afternoon watching TV in his Best Lane flat in Canterbury. He had been watching a lot of TV recently, grateful for some distraction, but it was too much for him to sit through the first week's tennis matches at Wimbledon: it caused him to question whether, at the ripe old age of forty-two, he was getting too old for racket sports. The severed tendon had surely been a sign. McGuire wasn't particularly sporty or a blokey pack animal who needed the company of other men, either at the gym or the pub. He was more a sociable loner who enjoyed his own company as much as that of others – and the odd game of squash until the injury had put paid to that. The enforced convalescence was difficult to cope with, not just because it had separated him from Pearl but because he'd had time to reflect on things he usually chose not to dwell on.

Due to cuts on the force, some of McGuire's fellow officers were accepting offers of early retirement at fifty and happily taking consultancy contracts, such as advising councils on safety for public events, like festivals. Retirement was something that McGuire had only ever been able to view as a final destination on a journey that had once seemed long but was becoming decidedly shorter. Though consultancy work was proving lucrative for some, McGuire had no desire to spend the rest of his working life having to deal with the kind of councillors Pearl had told him about – especially one dubbed Ratty Radcliffe – but if he accepted early retirement and eschewed consultancy, how on earth would he fill his days? By watching more TV?

The hospital had taken good care of him, with regular check-ups, and had adjusted the angle of his foot within the plaster so that the tendon was almost fully stretched, but they had also warned him that the recent spell of hot humid weather might cause his leg to swell: he would then need to rest it and keep it higher than his heart. Not wanting to do anything to impede his recovery, he had done precisely that, but now, after several weeks, he was in the mood to rebel. He wanted to go out and mix with other people – especially Pearl.

Switching off the TV, he turned to survey the view outside his window of the Great Stour River flowing fast below it. Across the water on a jetty beneath the terrace of an Italian restaurant, a family was being helped into a punt. The couple were in their early forties with two children. McGuire had always assumed he would one day have kids – most people did – though he had never regretted parenthood passing him by, only that the woman he had once expected to have a family with was no longer alive.

The death of his fiancée, Donna, had been a senseless loss, a shocking punctuation mark to a future that had once spread out in front of McGuire, like another long journey. It had ended, tragically and prematurely, with a fatal car accident in London. McGuire had sought escape – and a secondment to Canterbury had offered him that, but presented him with far more when Pearl had entered his life. Now he couldn't imagine life without her. It had seemed only natural that he should pose the one question he felt sure he needed to ask, and Pearl had accepted his proposal – though the wedding had been postponed, due to Pearl's numerous commitments and, latterly, to McGuire's accident. Life had its own way of throwing obstacles into his path – and the severed tendon was the latest.

McGuire's phone rang. 'How did your appointment go?' Pearl asked brightly.

'All fine,' said McGuire. 'Not much longer now,' he added, trying to appear positive about remaining in plaster.

'The time will go fast,' she said. 'Just keep doing whatever they tell you.'

McGuire couldn't hear any of the usual clatter of restaurant crockery and kitchen chatter on the line, so asked: 'Where are you?'

'On the beach,' she replied. 'And, in the words of the old postcard, wishing you were here.'

McGuire sighed. 'I'd get sand in my cast.'

'You know the beach here is pebbled.'

'Even more uncomfortable . . . Are you going sailing?'

He allowed himself to imagine Pearl out on the estuary water in her wooden dinghy with the breeze flowing through her long Gypsy-black hair, until she explained: 'It's low tide . . . We've got a problem down at the allotment.'

'Weeds?'

'Complaints. The council has sent letters to us. Someone's even been given an under-cultivation notice.'

'A what?'

'I looked up the regulations,' Pearl explained. 'Seems we're meant to be using at least sixty per cent of the land we're allotted or our agreements can be terminated.'

'Sounds reasonable.'

'Does it?'

'Use it or lose it?'

'Well,' said Pearl, 'I'd say this particular allotment holder, David Chappell, has already lost too much. His wife had an affair that's broken his heart and it's only recently that he felt able to return to his plot. Now he's about to have it taken from him.' She paused. 'I've finished at the restaurant for the day and I need to go and talk to him,' she explained, 'check that he's okay and still coming to an important meeting tonight.'

'Meeting?'

'It's been called by another allotment holder,' said Pearl, 'presumably to discuss all this.'

McGuire managed to stifle some resentment about Pearl meeting a man who had just been abandoned by his wife. Staring out of his window again, he noticed a couple climbing into another punt, sitting close to one another as the boatman took up his pole and launched the vessel from the quay.

'Are you still there?' asked Pearl.

'Sure,' McGuire replied softly, closing his eyes and thinking about suggesting something to her as he summoned up another image of Pearl beside him, her beautiful moonstone-grey eyes fixed on him as they glided along the Stour towards the setting sun. Then he opened his eyes and stared instead at the blue plaster on his leg, aware there was no way he would even be allowed onto the restaurant's jetty, let alone into a punt.

'Do you need anything?' she asked.

McGuire thought of the two things he needed most – a leg free of blue plaster and Pearl – but he said: 'I'm fine.' Then he tried to be magnanimous. 'That guy sounds like he could do with your help. I hope your meeting goes well, Pearl.'

On ending the call, McGuire tossed his phone onto the bed and switched on the TV again, only to find the evening news bulletin offering a report on today's action from the tennis played at Wimbledon.

After the call to McGuire, Pearl checked the time on her phone and decided to head off in the direction of town. Whitstable's tourist season seemed to grow longer each year, with visitors arriving as early as February to spend Valentine's breaks in the town's numerous B & Bs, including Dolly's Attic – the little flat above Dolly's Pots, from which Pearl's mother sold her seascapes and 'shabby chic' ceramics. For years, Pearl had served oysters on Dolly's distinctive plates but now they were being snapped up as fast as the oysters for which Whitstable had long been famous. The town and Pearl's restaurant were thriving but this new-found popularity had come at a price – not least because of the tension that existed between the DFLs and Whitstable natives.

On most summer days, locals like Pearl found themselves pushing against a tide of tourists heading towards the gift and coffee shops in Harbour Street, only to peel off towards the escape routes of ancient alleys, most of which had been constructed to give access to the town's main business place – the sea. Centuries ago, they had formed escape routes for smugglers but now townspeople relied on them to cut short their journeys.

Squeeze Gut Alley, as the name suggested, sliced a narrow route from the high street down to the stretch of road known as Island Wall where Pearl's own cottage was situated. At this hour, a hiatus always existed between daytime activities at the beach or in Harbour Street – a quiet spell during which parents would feed and bathe children while others would take a shower and dress for the evening before taking to the 'prom'. There they would saunter and swagger, enjoying a coastal view of such clear northern light that its skies and sunsets had been described by Turner, the painter, as 'some of the loveliest in Europe'.

Passing beneath the old railway bridge on Whitstable's Oxford Street, Pearl continued along Canterbury Road to David Chappell's home. Squeezed between two large houses, David and Cindy had bought the modest bungalow a few months before they had married. Although the property had seemed dull and old-fashioned at the time, David had undertaken a lot of work on it, and its old white stucco exterior was now painted a fashionable dull shade of green with lights mounted either side of the front door. The front garden had been laid to lawn, but as Pearl approached, she saw this had been left as untended as David's allotment, abandoned to a sea of small daisies and marigolds.

She rang the doorbell. No response. Moving to a side path leading to the back garden, a sight of similar neglect met her: David's rear garden had completely gone to seed. Pearl sighed, recalling his distress that morning had demonstrated his desire to hold on to his plot. Now she wondered how practicable that might be. Perhaps it would be better to persuade him to allow a group of volunteers to bring his allotment and his garden under control. If accomplished, perhaps the rest of David's life might follow. It would have been good to discuss this with him, and in particular, his outburst that morning, but the fact that he wasn't at home seemed to indicate that he had already set off to attend Caroline Lanzi's meeting.

Turning her back on the sorry state of David's garden, Pearl now decided to do the same.

CHAPTER FOUR

The Lanzis' home lay on the northern side of Joy Lane, a long road that began beyond an old toll-keeper's cottage at the entrance to the town, and continued in the direction of the village of Seasalter, two miles away on a link route that had existed for almost two hundred and fifty years. At that time, much of the land comprising Joy Lane had been leased by the founder of an infamous smuggling fraternity known as the Seasalter Company, which had regularly stage-managed the landing of illegal consignments of tobacco, brandy and perfume, with the nearby woods at Blean offering cover for the goods' eventual transportation to London. Decoy systems and elaborate signals involving lanterns in windows and broom-heads up chimneys had allowed the smugglers to play a cat-and-mouse game with the local excise men. Sometimes the authorities had won, and in 1780, a seventeen-year-old smugglers' accomplice had been executed, his body hung in chains on a gibbet.

Now it was a unique and desirable area of the town, especially as most of Joy Lane's properties had been built on generous plots that were coming under increased pressure for redevelopment for further housing. Homes were particularly sought after in this area, especially on the northern side where gardens, like that of the Lanzis, backed on to a spectacular coastal view.

Pearl remembered visiting the Lanzis' house when it had previously belonged to a local couple, an architect and his husband, who had spent a small fortune renovating the property and installing a swimming-pool on the lower part of a beautiful terraced garden. They had sold their dream home following an offer of work in California.

In spite of all the improvements they had made, as Pearl approached the house she could see that much had changed since the Lanzis had taken up residence. A substantial front garden, once filled with tall palms, had been flattened to make room for vehicles. Caroline's sleek convertible Porsche and Franco's silver Ferrari Purosangue SUV were parked in pride of place on a substantial forecourt, on which Pearl also spied Victor Bessant's Bentley Continental alongside Marty Smith's red MG. A bright green Citroën 2CV, belonging to Joe and Florence, was parked close to Michael's sensible Volvo estate, but Vanessa's Punto was absent, leading Pearl to suspect that the two had probably arrived together. Ted Rowden's mobility scooter was also on the forecourt but, with no sign of Dolly's Morris Minor,

Pearl assumed that her mother, as usual, would be the last to arrive, punctuality not being Dolly's strong point.

As Pearl climbed steps to a white stucco porch set with columns, she noted a sophisticated alarm system at the front door. Pressing the bell, she fixed her gaze on the camera lens, expecting a greeting from one of the Lanzis, though none was forthcoming. Then Caroline's voice sounded through the speaker, offering a curt instruction: 'Come through, please, Pearl. We're in the garden.'

The front door opened and Pearl made her way through a grand hallway and out onto a patio lit with decorative filament bulbs. Towards the rear of the garden, by the floodlit pool, Pearl caught sight of Franco pouring glasses of Prosecco. Ted Rowden was seated at a poolside table, sipping a slender glass of lager, while dressed rather unsuitably for such a warm evening in dark green corduroy trousers and a matching waistcoat over a gingham shirt that Pearl was sure he usually kept for gardening. In contrast, Marty Smith was perched on a stylish cantilevered chair, sporting a white dinner jacket, his dark hair gelled back as he sucked a green olive from the cocktail stick in his hand. '*Buenas noches, Pearl!*' he called, greeting her with a smug smile and a smarmy wink, a glass raised in his hand.

'Don't you mean *buona sera*?' said a puzzled Victor Bessant, sitting beside his wife Natasha, his hand stroking her knee.

Marty's smile faded. 'I don't know,' he said, sounding suddenly unsure. 'Do I?'

Michael and Vanessa stifled their amusement while Caroline gestured to a chair. 'Take a seat, Pearl,' she began. 'I'm guessing you'd like some Prosecco.' Pearl nodded, thanked her and noted that Joe and Florence were already sipping from sparkling flutes. The young couple looked out of place in their surroundings, with Joe in a white collarless shirt and torn jeans, his long black hair tied back in a ponytail, while Florence was wearing one of the pretty Bohemian-style dresses that she made from vintage floral-patterned scarves.

Pearl smiled at them both. They were an attractive couple, Florence's fragile fair beauty complementing Joe's dark good looks and soulful eyes.

Caroline went on: 'Your mother called a few moments ago, Pearl. She's on her way now with the other lady.'

'Madge,' said Ted, struggling with a piece of *bruschetta*.

'And David?' asked Pearl.

'Hopefully he'll be here soon,' said Caroline, as her husband handed Pearl a glass of Prosecco and a warm smile.

Pearl noted that Franco Lanzi was a conventionally handsome man with piercing ice-blue eyes and thick silver hair slicked back from his suntanned face. His body was toned and he seemed to possess a natural physical ease that must have served him well in his former career as a fashion model. His eyes seldom strayed from his wife, who was at least ten years his senior, but Caroline appeared well-preserved with wrinkle-free features and what seemed to Pearl an improbable pout. A loose taupe

46

trouser suit hung on her slender frame, silver bracelets jangling at her wrist as she raised her glass, exposing, or perhaps flaunting, a large diamond ring on her wedding finger that glinted beneath the pool terrace lights. 'Chin-chin!'

After everyone had taken a sip of their drinks, Michael fixed Pearl with a look and explained: 'Caroline was just telling us she had something important to discuss.'

'I'm sure,' said Pearl, 'or we wouldn't all be here.'

Before Caroline could respond, a rattling car exhaust shattered the peace. Caroline turned to her husband, but Franco was silenced by an engine backfiring.

'That'll be Dolly,' said Ted, unruffled, setting down his lager. 'You can hear her coming from miles away in that banger.' He shared a smile with Pearl while Franco responded to the doorbell.

A few moments later Dolly barrelled her way down the steps from the patio, Madge Tolliday behind her. Beneath the terrace lights and out of her Whitstable Pearl apron, Dolly appeared as an explosion of colour, in a paisley smock and a primrose-yellow turban from which a flash of newly coloured magenta fringe protruded. She waved to each of her allotment neighbours, showing off fingernails each painted a different colour. 'Sorry we're late.'

'I couldn't find my purse,' said Madge, offering a smile to Ted.

'You didn't need it, you daft Doris,' he said. 'Drinks are all free.'

He raised his glass, while Franco indicated a chair for Madge and a recliner for Dolly, but Pearl's mother was eyeing a wicker womb chair hanging from a nearby pergola. Making a beeline for it, she declared: 'I'll take this, if you don't mind. I had one of these back in the seventies.' Manoeuvring herself into it, she accepted a glass of Prosecco from Franco, taking a welcome sip before she asked: 'So what's all this about?'

Pearl gave Dolly a guarded look. 'David isn't here yet. We should wait for him.'

Caroline checked her watch and got to her feet. 'Actually, I think we've waited long enough,' she said briskly.

'I agree,' said Victor, seeming somewhat uncomfortable. 'I'm afraid Tash and I don't have long. We've a private view to get to this evening.'

Seemingly torn, Natasha Bessant glanced across at Caroline and Franco. 'You did say this was important, Caroline?'

'It certainly is,' said Madge, before either host could say a word. 'And we all know what it's about.'

Caroline seemed surprised. 'Really?'

'The allotment, of course,' said Ted, brushing *bruschetta* crumbs from his waistcoat.

Caroline and Franco met each other's eye before she replied. 'Well, of course, seeing as we're all allotment holders.' She checked her phone, this time betraying some irritation. 'But as David has chosen not to join us or to send his apologies, perhaps someone can explain to him tomorrow.'

'Explain what?' asked Pearl.

'My new plan,' Caroline said loftily. 'We need some improvements on the allotment site and, after much thought, I've decided to act on this.'

'So it seems,' said Michael, with a brooding look at Vanessa.

Caroline announced: 'An Allotment Association.'

Pearl turned to the other allotment holders and saw Ted Rowden's jaw drop open.

Caroline went on: 'There are some very good reasons why we should form one.'

'Like what?' asked Joe.

'For a start,' Caroline began, 'an association and regular meetings can provide a very good way to getting to know our fellow plot holders—'

'But we *already* know each other,' said Ted.

Madge jabbed a thumb in Ted's direction. 'He's right. Me and Ted have been friends for almost forty years.'

'Fifty, Madge,' Ted corrected her.

'Is it?' asked Madge, to which Ted gave a firm nod.

Caroline continued: 'I've been learning how some allotments have been lost to developments – and as there are plenty of those in Whitstable an association might help us to resist that, should we have to.'

'Admittedly,' said Pearl, 'that's a valid point.'

She turned to Dolly, who responded: 'But we don't need an association to do that.'

Caroline sighed. 'I was going to add that we can also share tips and experiences, and with regular meetings like this, we could properly discuss important issues and concerns, as well as the need to purchase some communal equipment.'

'We've already done that,' said Dolly. 'We clubbed together and bought that composter of yours.'

'*Ours*, Dolly, ours,' said Caroline. 'We bought it together, remember? And it isn't just *any* old composter, it's a *hot* composter. I did hand out full information about the use of carbon-rich ingredients, such as straw, corn stalks, small twigs, dry autumn leaves, as well as nitrogen-rich ingredients, like grass clippings, coffee grounds and tea bags. Whatever you use it's important to chop it finely so it breaks down as quickly as possible.' She gave a satisfied smile to which Ted reacted with an audible groan.

'Did you say something, Ted?' She gave him a hard stare. Ted shook his head, and Caroline continued: 'Well, the key to success with *hot* composting consists of two things: monitoring soil temperature and moisture *and* turning the compost regularly. Your information sheets explained all you need to know about checking the temperature. After three weeks of doing so, we should have a beautiful dark brown crumbly compost that we can all add to our soil.'

She gave another smile but this time Dolly offered a loud sigh and Ted followed with a grumble: 'We could have managed with the old pile.'

'We could,' Caroline agreed, 'but not half as well. You'll get used to the hot composter, Ted. It will be a great success and will benefit us *all*.'

'Ruddy great thing,' said Madge, speaking over Caroline.

Franco attempted to mediate. 'It's true that it's much larger than what was there before.'

Caroline went on: 'That's because it's going to provide us with *more* compost. As explained, all we have to do is to share the responsibility of monitoring the temperature and moisture levels, and the task of turning it regularly.'

'And the association?' said Pearl, returning to the matter in hand.

Caroline replied: 'No one needs to become heavily involved if they don't want to, but agreeing to become a paid-up member will mean that any funds raised can be used to benefit our site . . . Importantly, an association can also act as a voice for all members, liaising with the council should any problems arise.'

Dolly frowned. 'I see. And there seems to be only *one* voice doing all the talking here.'

'*And* to the council,' said Madge.

'Meaning?' said Caroline.

Michael Stopes took a deep breath. 'Look, there's no point in beating around the bush. Let's talk about the real reason we're here.'

Beside him, Vanessa found her voice. 'Michael's right,' she said. 'Why did you lodge those complaints, Caroline?'

'Complaints?' Caroline asked.

'And don't pretend you don't know,' Ted warned.

'We've all had letters from the council,' said Joe.

'Not *all* of us,' said Marty, accepting another cocktail from Franco. 'As I said this morning, those of us who *haven't* broken the rules haven't received any complaints.' He looked from Caroline to the Bessants.

Natasha seemed confused. 'I don't know anything about any complaints.'

'What a surprise!' said Dolly.

Ted leaned forward in his seat. 'And what about my bees?'

'What about them?' asked Caroline.

'And my hens?' said Vanessa.

Madge was scowling. 'I should be allowed to grow my grass as long as I like – and as for mosquitoes—'

'What on earth are you talking about?' asked Caroline, confounded.

'Don't try to play innocent,' said Madge.

'Please . . .' said Franco, trying to take control.

'Did you or did you not submit the complaints?' asked Michael.

Caroline looked bewildered. 'I haven't a clue what you're talking about.'

Pearl set down her glass. 'Then why did you invite us here tonight?'

'I just told you,' said Caroline. 'An association. We need one at the allotment. I've done all the necessary research – or, rather, my PA has – and I have all the information here for you.'

As she took a batch of paperwork from a folder, it was Pearl's turn to look confused. 'Are you saying you had absolutely nothing to do with the complaints that have been submitted?'

'That's exactly what I'm saying,' said Caroline, firmly.

At this, a silence fell. Victor Bessant checked his watch. 'We really have to go soon.'

His wife, Natasha, looked conflicted. 'I'm so sorry, Caroline,' she said, setting down her glass. 'I'm sure you're right about an association,' she went on. 'You're always right about everything.'

'Thank you, Tash,' Caroline replied with a smile, as she handed some paperwork to her. 'Do take a printout and read it as soon as possible.' She smiled at Victor Bessant and handed him a sheet. 'Victor?' Then, turning, she did the same to everyone, adding: 'I promised I'd keep Councillor Radcliffe informed.'

'Hah!' exclaimed Dolly. 'I might have known Ratty'd be involved in all this.'

Caroline frowned. 'Peter Radcliffe has actually been extremely helpful and agreed to facilitate our association.'

'We don't have one,' said Joe.

'Presumably we all have to agree to it first,' Florence said nervously.

'With a democratic vote,' said Pearl.

'But of course,' said Caroline. 'Democracy rules. We *must* vote to agree to it.'

'*Or* disagree,' said Pearl. She glanced around the Lanzis' garden, its minimalist style, concrete walkways framing patches of lawn and a sparse fountain. A question occurred to her. 'Can I ask why you need an allotment when you have all this land?'

'Of course,' said Caroline, unflustered. She indicated, for Pearl's benefit: 'We have a greenhouse for growing orchids, and the pool and terrace are quite expansive as you can see. A vegetable patch would be completely out of place, but as you know, the allotment is practically on our doorstep and I viewed becoming a plot holder as an opportunity to mix with other members of the community.'

'Mix with or meddle?' said Madge, under her breath.

Caroline went on: 'To share my expertise at improving our lot, or should I say plot, by liaising with the powers-that-be.'

'The council?' said Pearl.

'The local authority,' said Caroline.

'In other words,' said Dolly, 'Ratty Radcliffe – who, I expect, would be more than willing to get into bed with you.'

'*Per favore . . .*' protested Franco.

'Just an expression,' said Dolly.

Ted piped up: 'Allotments are not meant to be glorified gardens for those who already have them.' His gaze shifted from the Lanzis to the Bessants.

'Oh, I understand what you mean but I think that's unfair,' said Natasha.

'I agree,' said Victor. 'Tash and I have a small sea-facing garden on Island Wall – probably the same size as yours, Pearl.'

'That's right,' said Natasha. 'We wouldn't be able to grow much there and, besides, in the summer it's horribly overlooked by everyone on the beach – much like being in a goldfish bowl.'

Pearl was about to give her attention again to the conversation when she was diverted by what seemed like movement on the other side of the property's rear fence.

Dolly responded to Natasha: 'Maybe you should have thought of that before you bought it,' adding: 'Some of us have no choice. Ted, there, lives in a twelve-storey council block.'

'I know,' said Natasha. 'And I'm sorry.'

Victor Bessant sighed. 'Me too, for what it's worth. It must be awful living in that eyesore.' He turned to his wife and tapped his expensive watch. 'We really must go now.' The Bessants got to their feet while Pearl used the moment to keep her attention trained on the rear fence where she was sure the dark silhouette of a head was lowering out of sight.

The Bessants kissed the Lanzis, thanking them for their hospitality, while Dolly, having witnessed enough, attempted to get out of her seat – only to find herself wedged in it. She called in frustration: 'Pearl?'

Pearl turned back but before she could come to her mother's aid, Franco Lanzi was there, gallantly helping Dolly from the womb chair. Having done so, he offered a smile, which Dolly now returned, half charmed by Caroline's handsome husband. As the other guests got up to leave, Caroline said: 'I'm sure these complaints you spoke about can be settled amicably with the council.'

'We'll see,' said Pearl, turning to leave.

'Oh, and, Pearl?'

Pearl waited for Caroline to continue.

'The hot composter,' she went on. 'I drew up a roster for checking and turning it, remember?' She offered Pearl a copy. 'As far as I can see, it's your turn next.'

Pearl found herself silenced as Caroline handed her her roster. 'All the details are there,' she added. 'You can't go wrong.' She gave a satisfied sigh as Franco moved to her side and kissed his wife's temple. Pearl turned again to leave just as Caroline added, with the sweetest smile: 'And this week, if you don't mind?'

Straight after leaving the Lanzis' house, Pearl and Dolly stood on the forecourt, with the other allotment holders, and watched the Bessants driving off into the night in their Bentley Continental. Marty followed swiftly in his MG.

'Well!' exclaimed Dolly. 'What do you make of all that?' As Pearl turned to her, Dolly went on: 'She's lying, of course.'

Pearl glanced up at the security camera at the door and put a finger to her lips to silence Dolly, then turned to the others. 'I'll be in touch with you all tomorrow,' she said, '*and* David.'

They headed to their vehicles.

'Come on, Madge,' said Dolly, steering her friend across the forecourt to her aged Morris Minor. She turned back to Pearl. 'Want a lift?'

'I'm fine,' Pearl replied. 'I could do with a walk.'

She watched as Dolly got into her car with Madge, while Ted Rowden slipped his spectacles into his pocket and waved a farewell salute from his mobility scooter.

Pearl waited until everyone had driven away, then set off, heading back towards town along Joy Lane before she decided to take a dusty path, a public right of way that led to an area of the coast known as West Beach. The moon was rising as she continued, before taking another path that she knew would bring her back towards the rear of the Lanzis' property.

At the fence, Pearl watched the lights go out in the Lanzis' garden before she moved closer to the property's rear boundary, wondering if she had really seen someone lurking in this spot during the meeting. It seemed perfectly possible that the garden fence could be scaled, so perhaps she would mention to Caroline the need to increase security at the house.

Another thought occurred to her. Taking a step forward, she froze at the sound of movement among the shrubs that lined the pathway. Not rabbits at this hour, more likely a fox, or something else entirely. She whispered loudly: 'Who's there?'

The question met with no reply, only the sound of heavy footsteps scrambling down the embankment towards the railway line. Following, Pearl peered into the gloom to catch sight of a tall, hooded figure racing towards the old railway bridge that spanned the tracks towards the beach on the other side. It was impossible to be sure of the identity of the shadowy figure but a low rumble on the tracks signalled the approach of a train. It seemed to synchronise with the beat of Pearl's racing heart as she saw the figure glancing back in her direction just as the London-bound train thundered beneath the bridge, its lights creating a silhouette of the lone figure above it.

The hood of the jacket fell back with the force of the breeze. Immediately, the figure roughly pulled it up again, then hurried across the bridge to disappear down the steps on the other side. Pearl knew that a stretch of beach huts on the opposite embankment would offer the person more cover, but she felt no need to follow. She had seen enough to know that this had been none other than David Chappell.

CHAPTER FIVE

The next morning Pearl chalked up on her menu board the day's dishes at The Whitstable Pearl. They included fresh oysters and potted shrimps, tea-smoked trout and sea bass *ceviche* with a day-boat special of skate wing with black butter and capers. A morning spent shopping in Whitstable usually generated hearty appetites, and by lunchtime visitors would always be found huddling outside the town's eateries to peruse the menus on offer. Many would be seduced by the panoramic views of the beach-facing establishments but plenty fell for the charms of Pearl's restaurant, especially since it served the best seafood in town. Over the years, Pearl had developed her own recipes to satisfy tourists and locals alike, with a selection of signature dishes that included squid encased in a light chilli tempura batter, marinated *sashimi* of tuna, mackerel and wild salmon, and a popular staple of sardines cooked in chilli and garlic. One item always remained in popular demand, the delicacy that defined this little north Kent town, which might have gone unnoticed without it: its native oyster.

Pearl's staff were busy prepping. A new kitchen hand was helping chef Dean Samson to prepare an *escabeche* sauce as a marinade for swordfish steaks, while the young waitress Ruby was out on the restaurant floor laying tables. Dolly, whose culinary skills left much to be desired, was occupied in the safe but nonetheless essential duty of arranging table vases with Pearl's allotment sweet peas. Confident that all was in hand, Pearl took a break and headed towards Harbour Street while making a quick call to McGuire. It had become a daily ritual – and one that was necessary, though frustrating, because of late it always ended in the same way. After asking how McGuire was today, and discovering that he was much the same, she decided to vary things: 'Look, I have Dean cooking at the restaurant today so why don't you come over tonight? To the cottage,' she went on. 'I can drive over to Canterbury and pick you up.'

McGuire's reply took her by surprise. 'I could get a cab.'

Pearl was stopped in her tracks. 'You mean you'll come?'

'I can't resist your cooking any longer.'

Pearl smiled. 'Still no appetite for oysters?'

'You know I'm allergic.'

'So you claim. But not,' she added, 'to all Whitstable natives.'

McGuire smiled, well aware that the term extended to more than the town's oysters. 'That's true.'

'I'll come and pick you up at eight sharp,' said Pearl. 'The weather's fine so we can have supper on the patio.'

'Sounds great, Pearl,' he said. 'What are you up to today?'

'You first.'

'Right now,' began McGuire, 'I'm trying to get over the fact that DS Tony Hale has just been promoted to my patch.'

'Bad news?'

'There's a reason he's remained a DS for twenty years.'

'Until now, you mean?'

'Until I was stupid enough to have this accident.'

'Not stupid,' said Pearl, 'clumsy maybe.'

'Thanks.'

'Eight o'clock,' said Pearl.

'Promise you won't fuss?' McGuire heard a silence on the line. 'Pearl?'

'I promise,' said Pearl, as she ended the call, her eyes caught by something across the road. Tucked away in narrow Red Lion Lane, off Harbour Street, Franco Lanzi was standing with Natasha Bessant, holding her gaze intently and placing his hands on her shoulders as if to gain her full attention. Their faces were so close that Pearl felt they might be about to kiss, but instead Natasha shook her head slowly as if in answer to a question Franco had posed. In the next instant Franco moved off while Natasha appeared to remember where she was and seemed to brace herself before heading back across Harbour Street towards The Front.

A moment later Pearl followed, glancing into the Bessants' gallery window to see Natasha joining her husband, who was talking to a stylish couple apparently about a large abstract canvas on the gallery's rear wall. Pearl watched Victor slip an arm around his attractive young wife's slender waist, an action that seemed more proprietorial than affectionate as he failed to look at her. Pearl took a deep breath while trying to assimilate what she had just witnessed, then moved on, halting at the front door of the Old Captain's House, a fine piece of Georgian architecture situated just a few doors along from The Front.

White-walled and sporting mullion windows, the historic property had gained its name from a series of maritime owners, including one with connections to deep-sea diving, an industry Whitstable had pioneered in the nineteenth century after a local man had invented the diving helmet. That fact went largely uncommemorated in the town, apart from a few artefacts in the local museum and the naming of a local street as Dollar Row: its dwellings had been built following the salvage of a ship full of silver dollars. The Old Captain's House remained a reminder of that era while providing a suitable residence for Councillor Peter Radcliffe, from which he enjoyed lording it over the town.

Pearl rang the antique doorbell and waited for Radcliffe to open the front door. The councillor did so breezily, ushering her inside. 'Pearl,' Radcliffe exclaimed, in the strident voice he always used at council meetings. 'I got your text. You wanted to see me about something.' He peered at his watch. 'You're in luck,' he went on, 'though I have an appointment with the Sheriff of Kent at lunchtime – at the nineteenth hole,' he added, with a wink.

'Lucky you,' said Pearl, any hint of irony in her tone going unnoticed as Radcliffe led the way into the living room and out through its French windows onto a sunny patio.

He indicated a seat for Pearl at a wrought-iron table, then sat down, taking a handkerchief from his pocket to wipe his brow. It was moist with sweat, not from the heat of the summer day but the ill-fitting toupee he insisted on wearing. It provided a welcome diversion at local council meetings, and had contributed to his nickname of Ratty. 'Now,' he began, 'to what do I owe the pleasure? Something about allotment plots?'

'That's right,' said Pearl. 'A number of complaints have been lodged. Six allotment holders have received them.'

'Including you and your mother?'

Pearl nodded. 'But not the Bessants, your new neighbours, who own the gallery a few doors down, or Marty at Cornucopia or Caroline Lanzi, who I understand has been in talks with you recently about allotments.'

Radcliffe leaned back in his seat and gave a dreamy smile. 'Ah, Caroline.' He sighed. 'A remarkable lady and a wonderful addition to our community.'

'You think so?'

'But of course. Do you know she happened to represent the professional golfer Trevor Holstrom before he retired? And also that broadcaster and former MP who's made a terrific comeback after the "snouts in the trough" scandal?' He smiled again. 'He's back on our screens again, and all down to Caroline's management, I gather.'

'Really,' said Pearl, remaining unimpressed as she imagined Radcliffe pestering Caroline Lanzi for a few PR tips on his own political career – albeit at such a parochial level. 'Have you talked to Caroline recently?' she asked.

'I'm afraid not,' Radcliffe replied, 'though I know she was seeking my advice about the formation of an Allotment Association. A sound idea in my view.'

Pearl frowned. 'And what about the complaints?'

Radcliffe gave a shrug. 'I was entirely unaware of any until you mentioned them. And while I'm always happy to be consulted on local issues, as your elected representative *with* an increased majority,' he preened, 'you really should be taking this up with the relevant council officers. I'm sure any minor infringements can be resolved amicably.'

'I'm not so sure about that,' said Pearl, 'or that any "infringements" are considered "minor". One allotment holder has been served an under-cultivation notice and another accused of using a shed on his plot as a business premises.'

Radcliffe gave this a moment's consideration. 'There are procedures and regulations to be observed, Pearl. But I'm sure no action would be taken without the allotment holder at least being given a right to reply.'

'And what if they've failed to reply in time?'

Radcliffe frowned, but Pearl went on: 'One of our allotment neighbours has been very preoccupied with personal problems.'

Radcliffe gave Pearl a sidelong glance. 'Are you asking me to intervene with council procedures?'

'I'm asking whether Caroline Lanzi came to you for advice on how to lodge council complaints.'

Radcliffe's face set. 'And I've told you, Pearl, the only advice Mrs Lanzi has sought from me is about the formation of an Allotment Association.'

'Which you consider to be a "sound idea",' said Pearl. 'Particularly,' she added, 'should Caroline Lanzi become its chair.'

He took a moment to consider this. 'I can only say that, in my opinion, Mrs Lanzi would no doubt make an excellent chair. And *should* she take on that role,' he went on, 'I would be very happy to liaise with her on any matters pertaining to that association.'

Pearl sat back in her chair. 'Then maybe next you'll be recommending that she stands as a fellow councillor.'

Radcliffe's self-satisfied smile reappeared. 'Representing our constituents has always been a great honour, Pearl. Perhaps one day you might even consider standing yourself.'

'I'm not a politician.'

'True,' Radcliffe agreed, 'but I can tell you that I was only prompted to stand for public office after heeding Plato's words: "One of the penalties for refusing to participate in politics is that you end up being governed by your *inferiors.*"'

Pearl took her time to reply. 'Sadly,' she said, 'those in power too often represent their own interests rather than those they're meant to represent.' She paused, then gave a smile. 'Dolly Nolan.'

Radcliffe's lips tightened before he took a deep breath. 'I only wish that you and Dolly could appreciate the sort of improvements that new residents like Caroline Lanzi are keen to bring to our town.'

'Like helping the council with your plot-chopping? Subdividing so you can make more money from us all? Selling off land while promising to find alternative space elsewhere?' She added: 'Allotments should remain in the heart of the community.'

'They should also unite people of different ages and backgrounds, Pearl. So perhaps you should be more welcoming of Mrs Lanzi and what she's trying to do for you all.' Radcliffe paused. 'Do you know that during the Dig for Victory days of the 1940s, Britain had one and a half million allotments? But times have changed. Land is at a premium. Your plots were subdivided so that more residents could enjoy them. Equal opportunities, Pearl, something I would have thought you'd support.' He raised his eyebrows then went on: 'It was a fine idea of Mrs Lanzi's to suggest an Allotment Association.' He sighed. 'And it would have been nice to discuss that with her – and a few more of her ideas – this morning.'

Pearl frowned. 'What do you mean?'

'She was meant to meet me for breakfast. Now I'm beginning to think that perhaps you and your fellow allotment holders have scared her off.'

Pearl became suspicious. 'Is that what Caroline told you?'

'She hasn't told me anything,' said Radcliffe. 'She simply failed to arrive.'

Pearl smiled. 'You mean she stood you up?'

Radcliffe's lips pursed as he remained silent.

'What a shame,' said Pearl, offering him a sympathetic look as she picked up her bag to leave.

Radcliffe's voice sounded sternly behind her. 'Pearl?' She turned. 'This town has to move on. It's called progress.'

Pearl said nothing and simply took her leave.

A few hours later, after the lunchtime service at the restaurant, Pearl returned to Seaspray Cottage with some ingredients with which she planned to make a special treat for McGuire – a seafood quiche with shrimp and crab. It was one of his favourite dishes. As she worked in her home kitchen, the warm sun splashing across the patio and the drone of bees circling the lavender bushes near the open kitchen door, she hoped she might find time to dead-head a few geraniums. For now, while grating Gruyère cheese to spread on the top of her quiche, she listened to Dolly on speaker phone as her mother gave her verdict of Pearl's meeting with Peter Radcliffe that morning.

'So,' said Dolly, thoughtfully, 'Caroline's been ingratiating herself with Ratty.'

'And vice versa.' said Pearl.

'Yes . . .' Dolly mused. 'I can imagine how Ratty would like to crawl up Caroline Lanzi's begonias.'

'And what about David?' asked Pearl, changing the subject. 'Has anyone seen him today?' she asked cagily. She had not, as yet, told Dolly she had spotted David Chappell on the path at the rear of the Lanzis' garden the night before.

'No one,' said Dolly. 'If you ask me, he's gone to ground,' she went on, 'must be feeling victimised by that council letter.'

Pearl considered this. 'He was very upset when he showed that notice to me at the allotment yesterday. I wish he'd come to the meeting,' she added, still troubled by his absence.

'Maybe he didn't trust his temper with Caroline Lanzi,' ventured Dolly. 'To be honest, I was furious that she denied submitting those complaints.'

'Radcliffe denied it too.'

'He would.'

'So what do we do – about David, I mean?'

'Track him down,' said Dolly, 'and deal with that notice he's been sent. He's probably incapable of tackling it himself – and if he tries to, he'll only make matters worse.' She sighed. 'He's still not over things.'

'Cindy, you mean?'

'Of course. Poor man – but I have to say I feel sorry for them both. It was always a difficult match. David's so quiet and spends far too long on his computer – *and* everyone else's.'

'Well, that's his job,' said Pearl. 'He's an IT specialist.'

'I know, and it suits him. But his world grew smaller once he went freelance. He never coped well in social situations, even as a teenager, and a woman like Cindy Chappell needs attention – *and* a bit of fun. It was only a matter of time before someone like Russell the Muscle would come along and offer her that.'

A silence fell as Pearl placed her seafood quiche on the top shelf in her oven.

'I wonder where they are now,' she said.

'Spain, I believe,' Dolly replied. 'Marbella – or Marbs, as Russ always called it. He's been going there on holiday for a while. I wouldn't be surprised if he isn't looking for a way to move there. The property market's very lucrative, I hear.' She added: 'This allotment business has properly upset Madge too.'

'Oh?'

'Yes,' said Dolly. 'I got her back last night after that meeting only to find she'd forgotten her keys. I nearly called you for help – you've always managed to get into a locked door – but in the end I didn't need to as it turned out she keeps a spare set.'

'That's a relief,' said Pearl.

'Yes, except she couldn't remember where she put them. Well, not for a while anyway. We finally found them in the box that holds her gas meter by the front door.'

'Not a very safe place.'

'I agree. So I've taken charge of them now. Oh, and then there's Michael,' Dolly went on. 'He was on to me today about Caroline Lanzi. Said that something must be done about her – once and for all – because poor Vanessa's so upset about possibly losing her hens. She treats them like babies, but they seem to love her as much as the kids do at her nursery. Maybe they know she rescued them.'

'And maybe Michael wants to rescue Vanessa,' said Pearl. 'Those two are clearly becoming an item – if they're not already. Hold on a sec.' She moved to check the quiche in her oven.

'What're you doing?' asked Dolly.

'Cooking something special,' Pearl explained, 'for McGuire.' She smiled to herself. 'He's finally had enough of moping around in that cast and wants some company.'

'Probably only yours,' said Dolly. 'And about time too. Men usually go one way or the other when they're under par – either they want full nursing or the tough ones, like Mike, try to bluff it out. But he was never going to last without you for long.'

'I have to go, Mum. My other phone's ringing.'

'Charlie?'

'No. It's the mobile I use for the agency. Let's talk tomorrow!' With that, Pearl ended the call, wiped her hands on her chef's apron and picked up the mobile for Nolan's Agency. A man's deep voice sounded faintly on the line. 'Who is this?' asked Pearl.

This time the voice was more distinct – and familiar. 'It's Franco. Franco Lanzi. I need to see you.'

Pearl peered through the glass door of her oven at the surface of her quiche slowly browning inside. 'I'm afraid I've got my hands full at this moment, Franco.'

'It's urgent,' he insisted.

Pearl straightened. 'About the allotment?'

'About my wife. Caroline's disappeared.'

CHAPTER SIX

Franco Lanzi sat in the beach hut Pearl used as her agency office. No longer physically at ease, he looked bowed in his chair and diminished by worry, his silver hair dishevelled and his ice-blue eyes dull and swollen from lack of sleep.

'You say Caroline's gone missing?' said Pearl.

Franco nodded.

'Since when?'

'Since last night.' He clarified: 'After the meeting.' Restless, he got up and moved to the window, running a hand through his hair.

'What happened,' asked Pearl, 'after we left?'

Franco paused. 'What I tell you,' he began, 'will remain confidential?'

'Of course.'

Franco took a deep breath. 'We argued.'

Pearl allowed a moment to pass. 'About?'

Franco looked at her but remained silent.

73

Pearl went on: 'Look, if you need my help, you're going to have to be open with me.'

At this, he blinked, then returned to his chair. 'I told Caro she was spending too much time worrying about that allotment. It's not important.'

'It is to some,' said Pearl.

'I meant in relation to everything else.' He took his time before explaining. 'Caro and I have been together for twelve years. Married for eleven. And in all that time, she's worked hard to build up her business. Now she's winding it down, selling the company, and for the first time in years, we have the freedom to do all the things we always wanted to do, travel the world to places we've never seen or just stay at home and enjoy time together. But now she fills each day with petty . . .' He trailed off, seemingly lost for words.

'Council meetings?'

Another pause. Franco nodded slowly. 'I love my wife but in so many ways she drives me crazy, putting things like this between us.'

Pearl took this in. 'And what happened after this argument?'

He shrugged. 'She walked out. Left. I thought she was just going to get some air . . . that she needed some space.'

'She left the car?'

He nodded again. 'You saw she had been drinking so she would never have driven. I thought she might go down to the beach and cool off before coming back, but . . .'

74

'But?'

'I fell asleep on the sofa. I'd been drinking too. I woke some time later.'

'What time?'

'Around three a.m. It was still dark. I thought Caroline had come home and gone to bed, so I went upstairs. But she wasn't there. The bed hadn't been touched. She hadn't come home.'

Pearl saw fear in his eyes. 'Have you told the police?'

Franco shook his head.

'Why not?'

'Because I thought she might have gone to London. We still have a flat there. Caro could have called a cab . . . got herself an Uber. But . . . she's not there.'

'How do you know?'

'Her PA, Stella, has a key to the apartment. She checked for me.'

A silence fell.

'Could she be with friends?'

'Of course. But if she is, they're not telling me. That's why I need your help. My wife is trying to teach me a lesson. She's angry with me for the things I said. But it's hard. This was meant to be a new beginning for us in this beautiful new house by the sea . . . a proper home for us, instead of living out of suitcases and shuttling back and forth to London. We were going to relax . . . and make friends, not clients.'

'And you've done so,' said Pearl. 'You've made friends with Victor and Natasha. The Bessants?'

Franco said nothing.

'You know them well?' asked Pearl.

Franco gave a casual shrug. 'Victor was a client for a time.'

'But you and Caroline moved here first. The Bessants followed you to Whitstable?'

'Caroline told Victor about the Harbour Street property. He saw that it would be good for business, so he came down with Natasha. We had lunch together. Caro and I took them to the beach. She showed them a cottage for sale on Island Wall.'

'And your allotment?'

'The council had just made more plots available.'

Pearl thought. 'And suddenly they became your neighbours here?'

Franco inclined his head.

'Are you . . . close to the Bessants?'

'No, not close, just—' He checked himself, then explained: 'Look, I spoke to Natasha this morning and asked her if she had seen Caro.'

'And?'

'Not since last night.'

'And now you're here, worried that you've still not heard from her.'

'Of course,' he said. 'You have this agency. I thought if you made some enquiries, you could find out where she is . . . where she's gone. I can pay you – right now.' He reached quickly for his wallet but Pearl refused.

'That won't be necessary until I accept the case. But it would be helpful to have a list of contacts from you – friends, business associates, anyone she may have confided in or be staying with. Right now, I think you need to contact the police.'

'No,' said Franco, firmly.

Pearl spoke quickly. 'Almost a quarter of a million people go missing in this country every year. Most return within a few days but . . . some never do.'

Franco closed his eyes as if to blot out this fact. Then he opened them. 'I have to be careful,' he said. 'Caro wouldn't want the press to know about this. If she needs space from me, she can have it, but she wouldn't forgive me for bringing bad publicity to her or her clients.'

Pearl mulled this over. 'Okay.'

Franco Lanzi heaved a relieved sigh, then got to his feet. 'I'll go home and make a list of contacts for you. I can get that to you within an hour.'

'Good.'

Franco managed a smile and headed for the door where he turned back to Pearl. 'Thank you,' he said, and left.

Once he had left her office, Pearl found herself staring towards the window, catching sight of her new client mounting the small flight of steps from her garden to appear on the prom. Then he walked briskly in the direction of Joy Lane. In his place, a small fleet of dragon sailboats, looking much like white butterflies, drifted past on the tide as Pearl carefully considered all she had just heard.

Franco Lanzi had just offered the explanation she had been seeking all day, having seen him with Natasha Bessant that morning. It would account for the urgency Pearl had witnessed between the two but there seemed still to be something unaccounted for, something in the way Franco's hands had moved to Natasha's shoulders, in the look that had passed between them – or was it just unfounded suspicion on Pearl's part? She asked herself if Franco's explanation for having come to Pearl, and not the police, for help with his wife's disappearance was accurate – or could Natasha possibly have suggested it that morning?

Pearl tried to imagine McGuire's reaction to such an enquiry. It was true that people go missing all the time – temporarily, as most return – and a woman like Caroline Lanzi certainly had more than sufficient funds to stay in a hotel or even to catch a flight to some exotic hideaway on the other side of the world, but would she really have done so after an argument with her husband about something as trivial as a local allotment? Pearl watched the fleet of dragons and other sailboats disappearing past her window, then remembered she had to leave. McGuire would be waiting for her. She could ask his opinion when she reached him.

Exiting the beach hut, Pearl locked the door behind her and headed into her kitchen. Switching off the oven, she left the seafood quiche to cool while she placed a bottle of Chablis in the fridge – and checked that she had something else: Oyster Stout. It was McGuire's favourite beer and not easy to get hold of in Canterbury. Finding some, she smiled to herself, knowing he would appreciate it, then left.

In her Fiat, Pearl checked the clock on the dashboard, which showed the time as seven twenty-eight. If Franco was true to his word he would be sending through his list of contacts sometime after eight p.m. If the traffic wasn't too heavy, she would be back in Whitstable with McGuire by eight thirty and discussing Caroline Lanzi's disappearance with him over dinner. There might not be much he could do to help track down a missing woman but she would still be glad of his input.

As she started the car she ran through the conversation in her mind: *'Has she ever done anything like this before?'* Franco had offered no response to this other than a shake of his head. If the couple had been together for twelve years and married for eleven, why had this marital tiff been the one to provoke such a reaction in Caroline? Had Franco been telling the truth about the reasons for their disagreement? Was it possible that the cause of it was his response to the meeting, or that the couple had been spending more time together since their move to Whitstable – time that Caroline would previously have given to her work?

Pearl recognised that McGuire's enforced separation from policing had led to his own isolation, not wanting company – even Pearl's. It was true that some people lived to work rather than worked to live, though Pearl knew that she, too, enjoyed the daily challenges she encountered, both at the restaurant and at Nolan's Agency. Perhaps, she thought now, this was a result of hearing Dolly's maxim so many times: 'Busy people are happy people.' If this was true, was it also true that idle people were miserable? Was Caroline's interference in the allotment not so much inspired by her need to manage situations, and people, but a way of occupying herself? Could it also be true that Caroline hadn't submitted the complaints – but someone else had? And, if so, who?

Pearl's car slowed to a halt at the traffic lights near the old tollgate cottage. It was situated on an island in the centre of a busy road junction, a reminder that the route had once been a historic toll road when Whitstable had been developing as a seaside resort. In fact, the town had never adopted the more garish styles of nearby Margate or Herne Bay, remaining quintessentially a fishing town, which was still part of its abiding charm, especially with tourists. Pearl could see that the road ahead was congested with day-trippers heading back up Borstal Hill towards the motorway. Sensing she would be late for McGuire, she glanced towards the old tollgate cottage and acted on a sudden impulse, spinning her steering wheel to turn into Joy Lane.

What Pearl had suddenly realised was that if Caroline Lanzi had indeed been seeking some peace, and a refuge from her husband, a comfortable retreat lay only a few minutes from her home. A short while later, Pearl drove down the dusty path towards the parking spaces at Prospect Field. As with the local beach huts, it was against council regulations to spend the night at the allotments but Dolly had done so on a few occasions, with no one having discovered her, and surely Caroline might have found it possible to do the same.

Pearl parked and got out of her car, closing the driver's door quietly, before heading to the rusting gate. Once again, it opened beneath her hand, signalling that someone was already here. Starlings were swooping in a murmuration in the evening sky, before roosting. There was no sign of anyone working on the land as Pearl made her way to the Lanzi plot. As she trudged on, a few lines from a poem by Kipling echoed to her:

> *For where the old thick laurels grow, along the thin*
> *   red wall,*
> *You'll find the tool- and potting-sheds which are the*
> *   heart of all,*
> *The cold-frames and the hot-houses, the dungpits and*
> *   the tanks,*
> *The rollers, carts and drain-pipes, with the barrows*
> *   and the planks …*

Heading up a stone path of small bleached pebbles, Pearl called softly: 'Caroline? Are you there? It's me, Pearl.'

Silence.

Pearl now climbed two shallow steps to peer through the cabin's window and spied a stylish interior containing bookshelves, a small dining table, four bistro chairs and a wide sleeping berth covered with upholstery that matched a clutch of large cushions. No sign of Caroline Lanzi. Stepping away on the deck, Pearl leaned on a wooden railing and stared out across the plots. She knew it was too late for Ted Rowden still to be here as he usually made sure he had finished by seven to have his dinner at seven thirty on the dot. Vanessa's chickens were already roosting but Maggie's pond water gave a sudden gloop as a frog submerged.

Pearl felt thwarted. Checking her watch again, she saw it was almost seven fifty. McGuire would soon be wondering where she was. She thought to call him, then heard her phone signal the arrival of an email. Checking it, she noted it was from Franco, with his list of suggested contacts. Pearl surveyed the names and titles. They appeared to be mainly work colleagues with a few London friends but no family.

Scanning them, she became acutely aware that she was being watched. Keeping her eyes trained on the phone she braced herself and turned. Behind her, a sound near to the hot composter sent a flock of crows scattering into the sky. It seemed someone or something was heading quickly towards the embankment, though Pearl couldn't be sure if this was purely her imagination. Perhaps it was simply an animal that had been lurking, observing her from a distance – a fox attracted to Vanessa's hen coop. Equally, it occurred to her now that it might have been someone else – a disturbed soul, scared and perhaps needing help. She called towards the embankment: 'David?'

A sharp wind stirred the trees but no reply came. Birds began to re-settle and Pearl turned back towards the allotment, her gaze fixing on the expensive compost bin: a large trunk-shaped object the size of a hefty chest freezer, open at the top, with a trap door on its front. She reached into her bag for the paperwork Caroline had given her the night before – a roster and step-by-step instructions on how the compost should be turned while registering its optimal temperature for microbial activity. The sheets explained that the latter could be managed by using a soil thermometer or by plunging a hand into the pile. If it felt uncomfortably hot, it was sure to be at the right temperature, and hot enough to kill most weed seeds and harmful bacteria.

Pearl read on, learning that moisture was also essential, the contents of compost needing to feel like a well-wrung sponge. Too dry and microbial activity would be lost. Too wet and microbes could take over, resulting in bad odours and an almost complete stoppage of decomposition. If the pile was too dry, it should be given a good watering with a hose. If it was too wet, it should be turned, with some shredded newspaper or other high-carbon material added to soak up the excess moisture.

As Pearl read on she wondered how people like Caroline Lanzi could be so quick to assume leadership and dominance over others, imposing their own plans and orders upon them. Caroline's force of personality had taken the existing allotment holders by surprise. Caught off guard, they had failed to resist her insistence on this particular amenity and Pearl now saw that Dolly had been quite right: Caroline Lanzi's ambitions needed to be nipped in the bud. Perhaps a concerted vote against the proposal of an Allotment Association would be the first step towards this, a necessary symbol of resistance, which might prove enough to thwart further plans. If suitably frustrated in her ambitions, Caroline might then move on, as many DFLs did, once they tired of the novelty of living in a small town. Until then, Pearl would fulfil her own obligation regarding the compost roster, then mount her own objections in due course once Caroline had resurfaced.

Having finished reading the extensive instructions, Pearl now picked up a brand new spading fork that stood propped against the composter, ready to be plunged into the steaming contents. Her phone rang.

'Where are you?' McGuire asked, sounding unnerved and slightly miffed, as though anticipating that Pearl might not be coming after all. 'You said eight o'clock?'

'I know,' said Pearl, 'and I'm sorry. Something came up and I'm running a bit late but I'll explain when I get to you.'

McGuire's tone changed to one of concern. 'Are you okay?'

'Fine. I just have something to do, that's all. I'm down at the allotment.'

'Don't tell me,' said McGuire, 'you're bringing me a prize marrow.'

'Checking the temperature of a new compost bin. Hold on a sec, will you?'

She set the phone down, then grabbed the fork once more and began to raise it. McGuire's voice continued to sound from the phone. 'Pearl?'

'Hold on,' she called back. Thrusting the fork deep into the compost, she expected to have an easy job but found the tool met with some resistance. She withdrew it, stepping back as she decided to investigate by opening the hatch at the front of the cabinet. Immediately a batch of loose compost fell to her feet – followed by a pale hand.

At the sight of it, Pearl stood frozen, rooted to the spot, mesmerised by a diamond on the hand's ring finger, sparkling in the setting sun, just as Caroline Lanzi's had done beneath her terrace lighting only the night before. McGuire's voice sounded again from Pearl's phone – more insistent this time. 'Pearl?'

Ignoring him, Pearl clutched the garden fork and braced herself before lifting the heavy compost at the top of the chest and dumping it on the ground. A woman's face looked back at her. Caroline Lanzi's lifeless eyes stared up from a tomb of steaming compost. Unable to look away, Pearl picked up her phone with trembling hands and spoke into it without thought. 'I'm sorry,' she began automatically. 'I won't be coming to you after all.'

CHAPTER SEVEN

'You're a magnet for cadavers,' said Dolly, the next morning, in Pearl's sitting room as she handed her daughter a cup of dark liquid. Pearl eyed it warily. 'Go on,' Dolly ordered. 'Camomile's good for stress. You said you'd hardly slept all night.'

'That's true.' Pearl remembered waking several times from dreams in which she turned a steaming heap of compost to find Caroline Lanzi's face within it, the dead woman's eyes slowly opening as she spoke: *It's your turn next, Pearl . . . This week, if you don't mind . . .*

Dolly's voice broke the spell: 'Leave the restaurant to me and Dean, and take a good long rest today.'

'How can I?' said Pearl, in frustration.

'How can you not?' said Dolly. 'You're exhausted, and if news of this murder is leaked to the local press, you may end up saying something you'll regret. Then you'll get in the way of the police. What did Mike have to say?'

Pearl considered Dolly's question, recognising how far her mother had moved in accepting Mike McGuire in Pearl's life. Any man would have had to be special to gain her blessing where Pearl was concerned, but as a perpetual rebel, Dolly had always disliked the idea of authority figures. She had become disappointed with the police in particular when, some thirty years ago, she had failed to persuade them to join her in a protest at the Greenham Common women's peace camp.

Pearl gave a weary shrug. 'What could he say?' she said. 'There's someone else in charge of the case. Some newly appointed DI stepping into his shoes.'

'Ouch,' said Dolly, ominously. 'Rather him than me.'

'I broke the news to him on the phone last night,' said Pearl, 'and he called the emergency services.'

Dolly took a moment to process this. 'And bang went your evening together?'

'Of course.'

Dolly reflected on this. 'Did you happen to mention to the police what Caroline had been up to? The complaints and the plans for the association?'

'I had to,' said Pearl. 'They asked when I had last seen her alive. I was hardly going to lie about the meeting.'

Dolly bit her lip ruefully. 'Then presumably we're all suspects.'

'That's nonsense,' argued Pearl. 'No one could think that a complaint to the council about an allotment could possibly be reason to kill someone.'

'People have been killed for far less,' said Dolly, gravely.

Pearl knew she was right. 'But we don't even know that it was Caroline who lodged those complaints. She denied it, remember?'

'She would.'

'And the police won't confirm it was murder,' Pearl pointed out. 'Not until there's some proper autopsy reports.'

Dolly stared at her. 'You stabbed her with a pitchfork!'

'No,' said Pearl. 'It was the new spading fork that goes with the hot composter. *And* she was already dead.'

'Are you sure?'

'Of course! Why else d'you think her body had been dumped in the composter? The police will have to wait for an autopsy before coming up with an accurate time of death but we know for sure that Caroline was alive until the time we left the meeting. Then, according to Franco, she went missing.'

Dolly looked at Pearl. 'Do you believe him?'

Pearl met her mother's gaze. 'He also told me they had argued. Most murders are committed by the victim's spouse, close associates or friends.'

At that moment Pearl's cats, Sprat and his three-legged brother Pilchard, wandered across to greet Dolly, winding around her ankles until she began to stroke them. 'Did Caroline Lanzi have any friends?' she asked.

'Well, Victor and Natasha Bessant, for a start.'

'And why on earth would they want her dead?'

Pearl decided against telling Dolly that she'd seen Franco with Natasha the morning before. In the circumstances, it seemed a card best held close to her chest rather than to have this news broadcast to the town via Dolly's jungle telegraph – though Pearl now felt the need to disclose something else. 'I did tell the police that someone may have been there,' she began. 'Last night. At the allotment.'

Dolly looked suitably shocked. 'Who?'

'I don't know,' said Pearl, 'and I can't be sure . . .'

'But you have an idea?'

Before Pearl could respond, a ringing telephone broke the silence between them. She answered the call and heard McGuire's voice. 'I'll be with you in a few minutes.'

'But—'

The line went dead in Pearl's hand. She looked at Dolly, who got the message and quickly stood up, abandoning the needs of Pilchard and Sprat as she said: 'Leave the restaurant to me.'

It took McGuire ten minutes to arrive at Seaspray Cottage. Pearl opened the door to find a cab drawing away and McGuire, propped on crutches, on her doorstep. He was taken aback to see how drained she looked, the mischief gone from her eyes. 'Are you okay?' he asked gently.

Pearl managed a smile for him, aware that, as always, after a period of separation their reunion felt all the more intense. She took a step forward and threw her arms around him, holding him close, then breaking away just far enough for his lips to meet hers. Her gaze locked with his, and she noted that his blue eyes still held a sparkle, like sun on the sea.

'Well,' he said, with a smile, 'are you going to leave me here on the doorstep?'

Pearl stepped back and allowed him to enter, noticing the blue plaster cast protruding from one leg of his jeans as she observed his use of the crutches. 'You're surprisingly mobile,' she said, 'for Long John Silver.'

He settled in an armchair and allowed her to take the crutches from him. 'I can never leave you long without you finding a dead body.' He aimed a finger at her. 'If I didn't know you better, I'd have you down as prime suspect.'

'*If* you were in charge of the case,' said Pearl. 'But you're not.'

McGuire gave her a despondent look to which Pearl responded: 'If you will insist on playing squash.'

'It usually keeps me fit.'

'But now the new DI . . .' She struggled for a name.

'Hale.'

'. . . has been put in charge.'

McGuire nodded. 'You met him?'

'No. I gave a statement last night to a DS Bates, I think her name was.'

'Jackie,' said McGuire. 'She's a good officer.'

Pearl pictured the astute sergeant with beautiful green eyes and a charming smile. 'Pretty too.'

McGuire ignored this. 'I need you to be careful with Hale.'

'Why?'

'Because the man's an idiot, with a need to prove himself, and I don't want you falling victim to that.'

'I won't.'

'Good,' said McGuire. 'Then promise me you'll stay out of his way and not get caught up in this investigation?'

Pearl hesitated. 'I can't do that,' she said. 'This investigation is tied up with a case.'

McGuire sensed a familiar unsettling feeling coming over him. 'Case?' he echoed.

Pearl explained: 'Caroline Lanzi went missing two nights ago and her husband, Franco, asked me to find her.'

'Well, you did that,' said McGuire. 'You found her. Case closed.'

Pearl shook her head. 'You know as well as I do, it isn't as easy as that. Besides, Franco will need even more answers now.'

'If he doesn't already have them.' McGuire offered her a knowing look, which Pearl instantly understood.

'And what if he had nothing to do with Caroline's death?' she asked.

'The police will find out who did.'

'An "idiot" with "something to prove"?'

'Pearl . . .'

'Look, you can't ask me not to get involved. I *am* involved. I knew Caroline. I found her body.'

McGuire struggled with this. 'I'm sorry,' he said. 'It must have been a terrible shock.'

'It was,' said Pearl. 'If it hadn't been for Caroline insisting we should have that contraption at the allotment . . .'

'Contraption?' said McGuire, suitably mystified. 'A compost heap?'

'It's a little more sophisticated than that,' Pearl explained. 'Something called a hot composter. And it was my turn to check the temperature. Caroline reminded me only the night before.'

'Anyone there when she did?' asked McGuire, as he tried to find a comfortable position for his leg.

'All the allotment holders – except one. The meeting got a bit heated. Caroline could be really overbearing.'

'Enough to make someone want to kill her?'

Pearl thought back to the figure taking off towards the embankment trees. Was it possible that in his disturbed state of mind, David Chappell could have been moved to murder? 'I can't believe that's true,' she said. 'We were annoyed, resentful that Caroline might have complained to the council. Someone had lodged those complaints, though she denied she had done it. One person in particular was very upset about his notice.'

'Yes,' said McGuire, 'you mentioned that.'

'David Chappell's been struggling ever since his wife left him.'

'And how was he at the meeting?'

Pearl shook her head. 'He was the no-show. And he wasn't at home when I dropped by to see him. But . . .' She trailed off.

'But what?'

'Well, I may not have been alone at the allotment last night. When I got there the gate was open. I assumed that was down to Caroline but . . .'

McGuire followed her thread. 'It could have been one of the other allotment holders?'

Pearl nodded. 'Any one of them. We all have keys. Or it could have been a member of the public – *if* Caroline had left the gate unlocked.'

'Go on,' said McGuire.

Pearl fought a battle with herself, then admitted: 'I didn't tell the police that it could have been David.'

McGuire frowned. 'Why not?'

'Because it could just as well have been someone else. Forensics will surely turn up something.'

'On public land?' said McGuire. 'At a crime scene you contaminated by being there?'

'I didn't know I was about to find a body. I was on my way to you!'

'Via the allotment?'

'I just thought I'd check to see if she was there.'

'And you got your answer.'

Pearl moved closer to him. 'I'm sorry,' she said, gently teasing her fingers through his blond hair. 'I really wanted to see you.'

McGuire held her look. 'Bad timing as ever,' he said dolefully. 'You and I are always victims of it.'

'Except you're here now,' she said softly. She framed his face with her hand, amazed but reassured: there was something about McGuire that not only captivated but intrigued her – perhaps it was because in so many ways they were opposites, even in appearance. The Nolan genes of spirited Celt had produced a daughter with jet-black hair and moonstone-grey eyes while McGuire's cool Viking-blond good looks seemed somehow to match his more considered nature. For a moment, Pearl thought of Joe Fuller and Florence Brightling, another couple who perfectly complemented one another in their differences. 'I've got something for you,' she said suddenly. McGuire gave a slow smile and Pearl got to her feet, moving to the kitchen to return with a glass in one hand and a bottle in the other.

'Oyster Stout,' he said.

Pearl opened the bottle and carefully poured the dark beer into the glass. McGuire took a sip and felt himself relax, noticing the seascape beyond the windows before he looked at Pearl once more and began to lose himself in her eyes and the smile that made him forget the blue cast on his leg.

CHAPTER EIGHT

A few hours later, Pearl sat with McGuire at the patio table in her garden, which was set with her own take on a Florentine *panzanella* salad, featuring black olives and anchovies. McGuire watched as she poured two glasses of white wine, while they each thought of the special supper she had prepared the night before – the abandoned seafood quiche that had gone uneaten.

'So,' he began, 'if you hadn't headed off to that allotment last night, you would have arrived in Canterbury, picked me up and we'd have lived happily ever after.'

He sipped his wine while Pearl met his gaze. 'And I would never have found Caroline's body.'

McGuire picked up his fork and tucked into his salad. 'Your instincts were right about her being there.'

'But I expected to find her alive.' Pearl sipped her wine thoughtfully. Then: 'Perhaps it was down to Fate that she gave me the task of checking that composter or I'd still be going through the list of contacts Franco sent me.'

'Contacts?'

Pearl took out her smartphone and scanned the email he had sent. 'He expected me to check them out – to see if she'd been in touch with any of them.' She considered the list then shook her head. 'It appears no one saw her after she walked out on Franco two nights ago.'

McGuire sat back in his chair, enjoying the warm sun on his face as he mused, 'That's if she really did walk out.'

Pearl turned to him. 'He must have been telling the truth,' she said. 'The house has a security camera so your friend Hale is bound to view the footage from the previous night and confirm she left some time after the meeting.'

'And *arrived* at the allotment?'

'There's no CCTV there.'

McGuire picked up his glass. 'Then it's the perfect place to commit a murder. No immediate neighbours, plenty of tools . . .' He looked at her. 'Including a deadly garden fork.'

Pearl frowned. 'I had no idea it had been used to kill Caroline. I didn't see any blood on it, just . . . what looked like soil on the prongs.'

'Compost?'

'It's called a spading fork. Caroline insisted on buying it at the same time as the composter. She said it was good quality and would make easy work of forking over the compost.'

'Which presumably the murderer did after killing her,' said McGuire. 'She was buried in the stuff – effectively?'

Pearl nodded slowly.

'If you saw no sign of blood, it's likely she was stabbed with this spading fork,' said McGuire, 'then pushed back into the composter before the same tool was used to cover her body – with more compost?'

'Yes,' said Pearl, thoughtfully. 'Like pushing a body into an open grave and using a shovel to bury it.'

'Except you must have shown up on the scene shortly after she was killed. And you think someone was there?'

'I didn't see anyone. It was just a feeling I had. I've no idea who it might have been but—' She broke off, troubled.

'But what?'

'I did see David Chappell,' she admitted, 'the night before.' She added, 'After the meeting.'

'Go on.'

'He was on the path at the back of the Lanzis' property. He must've been spying on us over the fence because I thought I'd seen someone there. Straight after we all left, I headed down the same path to check I hadn't imagined it . . . He was still there when I arrived, but as soon as he heard me coming he took off for the railway bridge that leads across to West Beach.'

McGuire frowned. 'And you're sure it was him?'

Pearl nodded. 'I got a good look at him when the London train passed by – and his jacket hood fell back in the breeze.'

McGuire began to process this. 'Well, why was he there? And why didn't he come to the meeting?'

'I don't know. Maybe he just couldn't face it – but curiosity got the better of him.'

'Or maybe,' said McGuire, 'he didn't trust how he might act or . . . *react*.'

'He has a temper, yes,' Pearl admitted, 'but he's not a killer.'

McGuire eyed her. 'How well do you know him?'

Pearl looked away to avoid his watchful gaze.

'You didn't tell the police?' he said.

Pearl shook her head.

McGuire exhaled in frustration. 'Pearl, he was minutes from the allotment. If Caroline Lanzi *did* go there after the argument with her husband then Chappell could easily have followed – he would've *known* she was there.'

'But he *didn't* go there,' said Pearl. 'I just told you, he was heading in the direction of West Beach.'

'There's nothing to say he couldn't have gone back after you left. He could easily have returned, found Caroline Lanzi at the allotment, and you said yourself the man's got a temper . . . Maybe it finally got the better of him.'

Pearl said nothing as she tried to compute this.

McGuire went on: 'And no one's seen him since?'

'Not that I know of. But I told the police about the meeting at the Lanzis', what it was about and the complaints. They'll be interviewing everyone, and if Mum's right about David going to ground, they'll find him. I should call Franco.' She got to her feet but McGuire tried to stop her. 'Pearl—'

'He's my client and I need to talk to him.'

The doorbell rang, silencing them both.

'That's probably him now,' she said, relieved, as she turned to enter the house.

Inside the cottage Pearl moved swiftly through to the front door, aware that McGuire would find it hard to follow her. She was fully prepared to find Franco Lanzi on her doorstep but instead came face to face with a young woman.

'Pearl Nolan?' As she showed her ID, Pearl now registered a uniformed officer sitting in a car parked on the street. She gave a nod. The policewoman explained, 'We'd like you to come with us to the station.'

'Why?' Pearl asked. 'I've already given you a statement.'

'There's been a development.'

Pearl glanced back into the cottage to see McGuire still on the patio. She pulled the door closer to her as she asked: 'What kind of development?'

'We have a few more questions for you. Better we do this at the station.' The young officer indicated the car.

After a moment, Pearl reached a decision. 'All right, just give me a second.'

Stepping back into the cottage, she saw McGuire standing by the door to the patio. She went to him and picked up her bag but McGuire laid a hand on her arm and whispered urgently: 'You're entitled to a solicitor.'

Pearl nodded. 'I know.'

They held one another's gaze for a moment. Then Pearl managed a smile. 'I'll be fine.' She kissed him and turned for the door.

McGuire watched until Pearl had left. Then he looked back at the patio table – at yet another unfinished meal – and closed his eyes, cursing his disability.

CHAPTER NINE

Half an hour later, Pearl found herself seated at a table in an interview room at Canterbury police station. The atmosphere in the airless space was claustrophobic – reinforced by the hard stare DI Hale insisted on giving her through a mask of professionalism, which Pearl recognised was newly minted. She put him somewhere in his late forties, short in stature for a police officer and with a paunch she imagined might be the result of too many pub lunches. She noted the orange stain on his tie, which she surmised could be turmeric from a recent curry. Coupled with the absence of a ring on his wedding finger, she gained the impression that he was either single or possibly divorced. A tape machine was cued by the officer sitting beside him.

'Why have you brought me here?'

'You know why,' said Hale. 'It was made clear to you when you gave your statement that we might need to talk to you again.'

'That's right,' Pearl replied. 'But I don't have to answer questions without a solicitor present.'

'You haven't been arrested or charged,' Hale reminded her.

'All the same.'

At Pearl's challenging expression, Hale leaned back in his chair. 'If you prefer, we could always find a nice quiet cell for you while we wait for a duty solicitor to arrive. Is that really what you want?'

Pearl looked away in frustration.

'Good,' Hale continued. 'Then we'll continue, shall we?' He gave her another hard stare. 'I'm guessing you know that members of the public are obliged to cooperate with police investigations – particularly a murder investigation.'

'I know,' she said wearily. 'And I have.'

'Fully?'

'I gave a full statement last night to DS Bates after finding Caroline Lanzi's body. I was fingerprinted, questioned—'

'And why did you go to the allotment?' asked Hale.

'It's all in my statement. I'd been told by Caroline's husband, Franco, that she'd gone missing the night before. The allotment isn't far from her home. She has a studio on it. It's very comfortable. I put two and two together.'

'You were doing a favour for Franco Lanzi?'

'Not a favour. He hired me to find her.'

At this, Hale gave an amused smile and picked up a pencil from the table. He glanced towards the sealed window. 'Oh, that's right. You're not just any member of the public, are you?' He looked back at her. 'You're a private investigator – as well as a . . . cook?' He waited for Pearl's reply, softly tapping the top of the pencil against the table.

'I own The Whitstable Pearl,' she replied.

'So,' said Hale, 'why would someone more used to serving meals want to start up as a PI?' He shared a look with the sergeant beside him.

'I had some police training.'

'Ah,' said Hale, 'so you wanted to be a *real* detective?'

'A police detective,' said Pearl, 'at one time, yes.'

'And what happened? Couldn't go the course?' He smirked. 'Why did you give up, Ms Nolan?'

Pearl took a deep breath, trying not to rise to the bait. 'Personal reasons.'

Hale was still tapping his pencil on the table. The sound filled the silence. 'But you still fancy yourself as a detective? Playing cops between courses?'

On Pearl's silence, Hale leaned forward and turned the pages of a document before him. 'You've been involved in a few cases,' he went on. 'Is this one more to add to your name?'

'Why don't you ask me what you really need to know?' said Pearl.

'All right,' said Hale. Then: 'Why didn't you make a full disclosure last night?'

'What do you mean?'

'What *really* happened after that meeting at Caroline Lanzi's home?'

'I explained. We all left and went home.'

'So I'm told,' said Hale, 'by everyone who was there – including yourself. But that wasn't exactly what happened, was it? You lied about going home.' His eyes narrowed. 'Straight after that meeting you made your way along the public footpath to the rear of the Lanzis' home – on the other side of their garden fence.'

Pearl remained silent as she tried to compute something.

'So,' said Hale, 'what do you have to say now?'

Pearl spoke softly – almost to herself: 'I . . . was seen.'

'I take it that is an admission?' said Hale, confidently.

Pearl continued: 'David Chappell must have told you this.' Hale remained silent. She went on: 'Well, it's obvious. He was there – and he must have been there throughout the meeting that night.'

Hale exchanged another look with the officer beside him.

Pearl continued. 'I saw him,' she explained, 'except I didn't actually know it was David until I got a clear view of him on the railway bridge below the embankment. He took off as soon as he heard me coming. He must surely have told you this.' She waited for a reply that failed to come.

Instead, Hale asked: 'Why would you not mention any of this in your statement?'

Pearl looked away, then back at Hale. 'I . . . didn't think it was important.'

'Surely you know from your *police* training that it's not for witnesses to cherry-pick what information they give to a senior investigating officer.'

Pearl smiled. 'So I'm still a witness rather than a suspect?'

Hale tapped the pencil on the desk. 'You haven't answered my question.'

'Look,' said Pearl, 'I didn't want to implicate David unnecessarily. He's been having a tough time.'

'He's a friend of yours?'

'No. But he's a neighbour and a member of our community and I'd seen him only that morning at the allotment. He was upset about receiving a notice from the council. Someone had complained that he'd been neglecting his plot. Numerous complaints had been made. We assumed Caroline had lodged them, but she denied it at the meeting. David didn't come to it but I think he must have been listening in from the path.'

Hale fixed her with a look. 'And why would he do that?'

'Didn't you ask him?' Hale remained silent. Pearl explained, 'From where I was sitting in the garden, I became aware that someone might have been spying on us from the other side of that fence.'

'And did you happen to mention this to the Lanzis or to anyone else?'

Pearl shook her head. 'I couldn't be sure, and I only noticed this towards the end of the meeting, which was why I went to check.' She paused. 'David was there but he took off as soon as I arrived. I knew it was him as soon as he looked back at me from the bridge . . . Surely he's explained.'

Hale chose to ignore her question and broached another. 'In your statement last night you mentioned someone being at the allotment – just before you found the body.'

Pearl nodded. 'But I didn't see anyone. I just heard something or someone moving off towards the embankment – I could tell I hadn't imagined it by the reaction of the birds. They flew up into the trees as if disturbed by something.'

'Are you telling me this could have been Caroline Lanzi's killer?'

'I don't know. But if she was murdered just before I arrived it's a possibility. You must have an estimated time of death by now . . . Or would the heat from the composter have affected that?'

Hale studied her. 'Was it your belief that Caroline Lanzi submitted a complaint about your own plot?'

'Yes,' said Pearl, directly. 'But, as I said, she denied it.'

'And you believed her?'

'I don't know.'

'But you've had that plot for a long time.'

'It's in my mother's name – Dolly Nolan. It's a family plot—' She stopped as she realised something. 'I see. Method, motive, opportunity. That's what this is about, isn't it?'

'It's about you having lied in your statement.'

'I didn't exactly lie. It was an omission.'

'And I'm sure you're aware of the term "lying by omission",' said Hale. 'You stated you went straight home after the meeting. *That* was a lie.'

'And I *told* you why. I didn't want to implicate David—' Again Pearl broke off as she realised something else. 'But clearly David didn't mind implicating me. Why d'you think that might be?' She offered Hale a knowing smile, which was met only with a confused stare. She sat back in her chair. 'You know, if I'm the best you have in the way of a suspect, you really haven't got very far, have you?'

At this, Hale's lips tightened, a muscle tensing in his jaw. 'A warning, Ms Nolan. *Full* cooperation. *No* omissions. Or next time you might find yourself being arrested for obstructing an investigation.'

Pearl considered this. 'I'm not sure you'd be on safe ground,' she said smoothly.

Hale's brow furrowed. 'What?'

'Obstruction involves a positive and intentional attempt to deceive by wilfully giving false or misleading information. I think you'll find that's the principle enshrined in the 1966 High Court judgment of Rice versus Connolly.'

Hale indicated to the DS beside him to terminate the interview, then got to his feet, tossed his card onto the table in front of Pearl, and ordered, 'Get Ms Nolan home, will you?'

On returning to Island Wall, Pearl decided she needed to walk on the beach for some fresh air before returning to Seaspray Cottage. Gazing out towards the horizon she saw the tide had retreated, exposing a vast expanse of mud flats. In the hazy sunlight, hunched figures were visible though not clearly discernible – fishermen collecting bait, or small children searching for crabs, perhaps more successful in their efforts than Pearl in uncovering clues to Caroline Lanzi's death.

She went over her interview with Hale, recognising that David Chappell had clearly told the police about seeing her on the path near the Lanzis' home – but had he done so to offer a truthful account of his movements, or because he felt the need to implicate someone else? Had he suspected Pearl's motives for being there? Or was he more interested in transferring any suspicion to her? Pearl watched the shadowy figures on the flats and allowed herself to ask: could David Chappell really have killed Caroline Lanzi? The figures offered no clues. Instead they seemed only to become hazier, as dark clouds drifted in. Pearl knew they might pass with a stiffening offshore breeze, but with a change of wind direction, they could yet bring stormy weather. Pearl took a deep breath and prepared herself for more questions – this time from McGuire.

She descended the small flight of steps into her garden and unlocked the kitchen door. There was no sign of McGuire on the lower floor so she called his name.

Silence.

Putting her bag on the dining table, she saw what appeared to be a hastily scribbled note in McGuire's handwriting: 'I'll call you.'

In the next instant, her phone rang. Automatically she replied, expecting to hear McGuire's voice – only to find it was Franco Lanzi. He spoke urgently. 'I need to see you.'

Pearl stared towards the window as the first splashes of rain landed on the lead panes. A storm was on its way.

CHAPTER TEN

'This is a living nightmare,' said Franco Lanzi in a shocked whisper. 'Caro was sitting where you are right now.' Pearl could see he was staring intently at her – almost through her – as though he was looking at his wife sitting opposite him on one of two long white sofas in their beautiful home.

'You mean,' Pearl began, 'when you argued?'

Franco hung his head. Beside him, Natasha Bessant laid a comforting hand on his. Pearl noted it was trembling. 'It's a terrible thing,' Natasha whispered, looking to Pearl for a response, but it was Victor Bessant, standing behind them both, who replied.

'And the work of a maniac,' he said. 'We all argue with those we love. It means nothing.'

Pearl asked: 'You've talked to the police?'

Franco raised his head. 'Of course.'

Natasha spoke. 'We've given statements.'

'They interviewed us all,' said Victor, 'after hearing about that bloody meeting.'

Franco explained more calmly: 'They're talking to everyone who might have seen or heard from Caro recently.'

'Those names on the list you gave me?' asked Pearl.

Franco nodded. 'No one's been able to help.'

'As yet,' said Pearl.

'What do you mean?' asked Natasha.

'It's the start of a process of elimination,' said Pearl. 'The police will need to go through statements and check everyone's movements and alibis against the time of death.'

'They know ours,' said Victor. 'Tash and I were at home.'

'Nevertheless, you should be prepared for more questions,' said Pearl. 'I've just come from the station myself.'

'They took you in again?' asked Franco. 'Why?'

'A few things they needed to check,' said Pearl, guardedly.

'And do you know if they've told the press?' asked Franco.

Pearl shook her head. 'If they had, reporters would surely have been in touch.'

'Pearl's right,' said Victor. 'And the last thing Franco needs right now is the gutter press showing up with paps.' He checked his watch and seemed torn. 'I'm sorry, Franco, but Tash and I really have to go.' He nodded towards the hallway but Natasha looked back at Franco.

He managed a smile for her. 'It's all right,' he said. 'Go on. I need to talk to Pearl.'

Natasha got to her feet and picked up her bag. As she moved to her husband, Victor slipped his arm around her waist, and acknowledged Pearl before steering Natasha to the door.

Franco waited until he had heard the front door close after the Bessants before he turned back to Pearl and seemed to compose himself. 'I hired you to find Caro.'

'I know.'

'And you did that.'

'But not in the way either of us expected.'

'All the same,' said Franco, 'you did it. I owe you.'

'Not any more—'

'Listen to me,' he interrupted urgently. 'We had a deal, Pearl. And now I have a new one for you.'

Pearl saw that in Franco's face determination had replaced sorrow.

'I want you to find my wife's killer.'

'Franco—'

'I don't care what it costs or how long it takes. But I need you to do this for me.'

Pearl looked away, words from her earlier conversation with McGuire now echoing. *'Franco will want even more answers now . . . if he doesn't already have them . . . Promise me you'll stay out of his way and not get caught up in this investigation . . . You found her. Case closed . . .'*

Pearl fought with something inside herself. 'The police will do it.'

'And what if they don't?' he asked. 'If they can't?'

Pearl looked at him.

'Please?' he asked, softly now. 'Help me?'

Pearl saw Franco Lanzi's hands were clasped tightly in front of him, as if in prayer. She found herself agreeing to his request.

Ten minutes later, Pearl walked out of the Lanzis' home. Gathering her thoughts, she set off in the direction of the town while she checked her phone. She had had no calls or messages from McGuire and wondered whether he could have left his curt note in a fit of pique. Then she thought again, choosing instead to believe that the note had been written in a hurry because there was something important he had to do.

She had just decided to call him when she found herself staring up at the sign for the public footpath to the embankment. Casting her mind back to the night of the meeting at the Lanzis' house, she decided there was something she also needed to do – right now.

It wasn't long before Pearl found herself on the doorstep of David Chappell's bungalow in Canterbury Road. Pressing the doorbell she waited for a response. It failed to come. Once more she decided to investigate the rear of the property, hoping David might be there – only to find the back garden as empty and overgrown as it had appeared only two days ago. Two mornings ago, Pearl's only concern had been finding a way to persuade McGuire to emerge from his Canterbury man-cave, to stop feeling sorry for himself and rejoin the rest of the world. But the discovery of the complaints to the local council had been followed swiftly by the murder of a DFL – the same woman who had denied lodging the complaints. Could Caroline Lanzi have been telling the truth?

Moving to the back door of David Chappell's bunga-low, Pearl peered through a glass panel to view an empty kitchen. Dishes were piled high in the sink while a laptop sat on the table beside a highball glass and what looked, from a distance, to be a bottle of Scotch. Pearl sighed and moved away from the door to catch sight of a set of boxes used for recycling. Two in particular captured her attention: red for paper, blue for glass. Inside the red container she found nothing significant, just a stack of old newspapers and some magazines specialising in computers. Replacing the lid she now investigated the blue box, opening this to find it crammed with empty single-malt whisky bottles. She looked again through the kitchen door, eyeing the bottle on the table, which would surely be joining the collection before long. Perhaps David Chappell's recent isolation might not have been due solely to Cindy's desertion but because he had acquired a dependence on alcohol.

Staring across the garden, Pearl's gaze now settled on an old garden shed, which caused her to recall the state of David's neglected allotment plot. It was clear Caroline Lanzi had been murdered with the spading fork she had insisted on purchasing for use with the hot composter. It now also appeared to Pearl to have been an opportunistic crime – with the killer having come across Caroline at the allotment that evening, perhaps someone who had taken issue with her about the complaints. David had already demonstrated his rage to Pearl – a man brought to a tipping point by recent events: could they have proved to be a sufficient motive for murder? If David Chappell had indeed killed Caroline and taken off just as Pearl had arrived, why had he made sure to inform the investigating police officer that Pearl had been lurking at the rear of the Lanzis' property after the meeting? Was his intention to incriminate her while absolving himself?

As Pearl mulled it over, she accepted that McGuire had been right: she should have disclosed this in her own statement to the police instead of handing DI Hale something he might well choose to use against her and, by implication, McGuire.

Pearl crossed the garden to the shed and reached for the door handle. She was unsure what she might find within – more evidence of David's drinking or another gruesome discovery? As her hand closed tightly around it, she was reminded of a portrait that hung in the Beaney Museum in Canterbury. It was a portrait by Harriet Halhed, *The Little Girl at the Door*, which showed a child, dressed in a black hat, winter coat and polished boots, her hands clenched around the brass knob of an imposing grey door as she stared back towards the viewer, unsure of what, or whom, she might find on the other side. It was an image that had never failed to intrigue Pearl because the door in the portrait remained for ever closed. Countless times throughout her childhood she had imagined what she might have encountered if the door had opened and had always felt strangely connected to the girl, needing to open the door and solve the unsolved mystery . . .

Gripping the handle, Pearl prepared to yank open the shed door when a voice behind her asked, 'What do you think you're doing?'

Pearl wheeled round and came face to face with a figure wearing a familiar hooded jacket. David Chappell held Pearl's eyes as he waited for her reply.

CHAPTER ELEVEN

McGuire stood at the window of his Canterbury flat, carefully scanning his phone for signs of incoming emails. He had wasted no time after Pearl had been taken in for more police questioning and had put in calls to a few trusted officers. Although he always wore the distinctive badge of a DFL detective in a county force, he had earned himself some reliable friends and colleagues at Canterbury CID. DS Jackie Bates was one. She was clearly part of the investigation, having taken Pearl's statement the previous night. Now she wasn't answering McGuire's calls, which signalled to him that she was already busy with the Lanzi case.

The first twenty-four hours in any murder investigation were always vital for obtaining clues, but the first sixty minutes after the discovery of a body were the most crucial – the Golden Hour – in which important evidence might be preserved. It was true that Pearl had forensically contaminated the scene of crime but she had been right in pointing out to McGuire that she couldn't possibly have expected to find Caroline Lanzi's corpse buried under a steaming heap of compost. Perhaps the body would still have been there, to be discovered by someone else, had Pearl not acted on instinct and made a detour to the allotment on her way to pick up McGuire. Worst of all for McGuire was that Pearl was not only now embroiled in the mystery but appeared to have become a possible suspect in a case assigned to Hale, of all people, rather than McGuire himself.

McGuire's relationship with Pearl had never run smoothly. Aside from the inherently problematic nature of an association between police officer and private eye, Pearl had always shown herself to be feisty, competitive and stubborn. McGuire, however, had been smart enough to recognise these as pejorative terms for what might, in a crime scenario, be considered as admirable traits. Pearl was also brave and persevering, which, placed in the context of a police career, would have made her an excellent officer, not least because, as McGuire knew only too well, most murders were solved by dogged perseverance. Although he was no chauvinist, McGuire would have preferred to meet Pearl in the role of detective sergeant, someone who, like Bates, would report to him and not dominate him. Instead, it was clear that while Pearl might well consider herself to be McGuire's equal, she would never settle for being his inferior.

Furthermore, while Pearl still seemed intent on satisfying an early dream, at the end of the day she was a restaurant owner with a sideline involving local crime, a small-town local detective. For that reason, her connection to a senior officer involved in the investigation of a serious crime had come under scrutiny from McGuire's superiors. While conducting his own homicide cases, McGuire had been forced to handle information from Pearl very carefully: the relationships between officers and informants were always strictly regulated and monitored – in theory at least. McGuire's own superior, Maurice Welch, had always shown himself to favour his own local officers over a Londoner like McGuire – although McGuire had spent almost two decades in the Metropolitan force. Welch was a small man in every way, his intelligence limited by a narrow viewpoint that rarely allowed him to see the bigger picture. He had played a good game of politics within the force, though, and had manoeuvred himself into the rank of superintendent rather than having earned it. Welch was no more than a big fish in a small pond but he had no wish to be reminded of it – especially by McGuire – and he therefore found McGuire's presence at the station irksome, perhaps especially because the new officer had a good record of solving murder cases.

An officer's successes still reflected positively on Welch and McGuire recognised he had to walk a tightrope in his new post. Welch might be happy to see the DFL detective gone, but McGuire had no intention of going. He lived for his job – and he was not about to risk it without good cause. He also knew he couldn't be parted from Pearl and, in turn, she would find it hard to leave

Whitstable for London, even for McGuire. He now took time to reflect on how Welch had seen that Pearl was his Achilles heel and he knew that, yet again, he would have to tread carefully, particularly as he was excluded from the official investigation, which Hale would use to prove his own worth.

After leaving a comprehensive message for Jackie Bates, consisting of carefully worded enquiries that McGuire hoped would be answered before long, he dialled another number, this time a contact in Forensics. McGuire was owed more than a few favours in the department and clung to the hope that Dr Aram Rawf would come through for him. Finally, he rang Pearl, hoping she had been released from custody. On reaching her voicemail he feared that Hale was still wasting valuable time asking questions of the wrong person. As he rang off, one question now resonated: if Pearl wasn't with Hale, where the hell was she?

At exactly the same time, David Chappell looked Pearl in the eye, wanting to be sure that her caller had rung off, before he reached for the Scotch bottle on his table and set it aside on the kitchen counter. He shrugged off his jacket and tossed it onto a chair. 'Sit down.'

Pearl took a seat at the table and Chappell did the same. 'Well?' he asked. 'Are you going to tell me what you're doing snooping around?'

'I came to talk to you,' Pearl explained, 'I was with the police again today. They wanted to question me after you told them I'd been on the public footpath near the Lanzis' house.'

'You mean you *didn't* tell them?'

Pearl shook her head. David's eyes narrowed with sudden suspicion. 'Why not?'

She sighed. 'Strange though it may seem to you, I didn't want to tell them anything that might incriminate you.'

'Well, what did you think I was doing there?'

'I didn't know,' said Pearl. 'Why don't you tell me?'

David looked tense, his lips pursed, staring at her in silence.

Pearl went on: 'You chose not to come to the meeting, but I was sure I saw someone at the fence while we were in the garden.'

'And you told the police that?'

'Why didn't you come to the meeting?' asked Pearl.

David wiped his face with his hand. 'I just couldn't face it. I've hardly seen anyone lately. The idea of being there, with you all . . . with that woman, everyone knowing what had happened . . .'

'You mean Cindy?'

He nodded slowly. 'I stopped going out in town a while ago. I saw the looks people were giving me.'

'What looks?'

'I knew what they were thinking,' Chappell replied bitterly. 'There goes the fool whose wife ran off with another man. The last one to know what was going on. The last one to know she was leaving . . .' He paused. 'Everyone was laughing behind my back.'

'No,' said Pearl. 'You misunderstood. People care about you. They feel for you.'

'*Pity* me, you mean?' he said sharply. 'The betrayed husband? The cuckold?'

He shook his head. 'I was wrong to think it could ever work between Cindy and me, but in the beginning it did. We were happy. At least I was. And if Cindy was unhappy she never let me know. She wanted us to buy this place together, and once we did I took on more work to get it just the way she wanted it. I didn't have much spare time so we couldn't go out much or take a holiday . . .'

'Cindy was working too,' said Pearl.

David nodded. 'At the Marine Hotel in Tankerton. First in the restaurant, then the bar. It's a nice place. She liked it there, but *he* was working on a house nearby, on Marine Parade, and then she started doing extra shifts. I was still busy with clients. Designing websites, dealing with queries . . .' He scowled at his laptop. 'I was plugged into this thing all day and most evenings. Computers. I've always known where I was with them. You can program them to do what you want.'

'But Cindy didn't do what you wanted?'

David looked away. 'I begged her to stay. I swore we could start again, that I would change. But it was too late. She said her mind was made up. They were going away together. Spain?' He gave her a dark look. 'I haven't heard from her since. Not a word. I tried to track her down online but nothing. They've vanished, and now there's just a gaping hole in my life.'

Pearl met his gaze. 'And in your heart?' she said softly.

David frowned again, this time as though he was trying to organise his thoughts. 'It's . . . true I wanted to have things out with Caroline Lanzi. All those complaints? I just didn't want to have to sit there through that meeting with everyone pitying me.'

Pearl watched him wringing his hands before he began to pick at his cuticles. 'You wanted to talk to her in private instead?' she asked.

'Yes!' he blurted. 'But I still wanted to know what she was telling you at the meeting. And I heard her denying it all. But I knew she was lying. She had us where she wanted us – on the back foot with the council – while she was cosying up to councillors like Radcliffe, putting that association in place so she could control everything and everyone. No hens, no honey, no unruly plots. Just the world as Caroline Lanzi wanted it.'

'And did you get a chance to tell her that?'

David looked sharply at her. 'What do you mean?'

'You said you wanted to tell her this in private, so did you call her? Meet her?'

He looked lost. 'How could I? She was murdered. I didn't get a chance.'

Pearl's eyes shifted to the Scotch bottle on the counter. 'Are you sure you didn't call her? You had her mobile number from the text she sent to us all.'

'No,' he said. 'I didn't call anyone. I came straight home after you saw me on the path. You *did* know it was me?'

'I knew,' said Pearl.

David swallowed hard. 'Then I suppose I should thank you for not telling the police,' he began, 'but I *had* to tell them myself. They cautioned me. I couldn't lie.' He went on: 'Do you think they believe I could have killed Caroline?'

'I don't know,' Pearl replied. 'Do you have an alibi for the time of the murder?'

'Last night? I was here.'

'Can anyone confirm that?'

David shook his head – defeated.

'Well,' said Pearl, 'if it's any consolation I'd imagine every allotment holder who received a complaint is a potential suspect, as well as those who were close to Caroline.'

David raised his gaze. 'Her husband, you mean?'

Pearl said only: 'Most murder victims are known to their killers.'

David took a moment to process this, then asked: 'What now?'

'The police will be doing all they can to track down more suspects. There'll be CID meetings to collate information and the allotment will have been sealed off until all the results are back from the forensics team. They'll also be awaiting the results of a formal post-mortem. That should give a more accurate time of death.'

'But it was you who found the body?' said David.

Pearl nodded. 'Just after eight p.m. I'm not sure how long Caroline had been dead. The heat from the composter might complicate things.'

David said, with new urgency: 'I didn't kill her. I swear.' He looked helplessly at Pearl. 'What should I do now?'

Pearl glanced towards the Scotch bottle. 'Keep a clear head,' she began, 'because you'll need your wits about you. Try to trust people again.' Leaning back in her chair, another thought came to her. 'There's a fundraising event tomorrow night. It might be good for you to come along and feel part of the community again, especially now.'

David Chappell took time to consider this. Finally he agreed: 'I'll try.'

Within half an hour, Pearl had arrived home to find Seaspray Cottage unbearably stuffy. This was often the case during the summer when a fresh morning breeze blowing in from the sea became increasingly laden as the day wore on, filling with the heavy aroma of barbecued fish and seafood before night fell. She went straight to her kitchen, unlocked the French windows and stepped out onto the patio to gaze towards the coastline. The navigation lights of freighters were already twinkling, like a string of precious stones – rubies, emeralds and diamonds. Jazz was sounding faintly from the Old Neptune across the beach.

Taking her phone from her bag Pearl checked it and found a text from Dolly, confirming that last orders had been served at the restaurant. There was also a missed call from McGuire – the one she had been unable to accept when David Chappell had caught her in his garden. She dialled McGuire, expecting him to answer straight away, but instead it took him a while to respond. He did so with a formal 'McGuire.'

Pearl frowned. 'You're there,' she said. 'Hale released me earlier.'

'I know,' said McGuire. 'I'm with a colleague.'

'You're off work at the moment,' she reminded him, 'and meant to be taking it easy.'

McGuire spoke quickly. 'I've made some enquiries.' Pearl registered the tone he was using – professional: short staccato phrases that never strayed from the point. They had to be for someone else's benefit.

'Who are you with?' she asked curiously.

'I can't say.'

'DS Bates, by any chance?'

'That's right.'

'I see.' Pearl imagined him with the woman to whom she had given her statement last night: an attractive colleague, someone he clearly trusted, but a stranger to Pearl.

'Are you okay?' he asked.

Pearl closed her eyes to the sight before her – the coastline darkening – then turned her face to the warm evening breeze, allowing it to kiss her cheek and wishing it was McGuire.

'Pearl?'

Opening her eyes she replied, 'I'm fine.'

'Good,' said McGuire. 'We'll talk tomorrow. I should have some answers then.'

The line clicked off. McGuire's voice was replaced with the lapping of a retreating tide.

CHAPTER TWELVE

The next morning, Pearl peered around The Whitstable Pearl's kitchen door. Her fellow allotment holders – Joe and Florence, Michael and Vanessa, Ted Rowden and Madge Tolliday – sat at one of the tables. Turning back to Dolly, Pearl whispered: 'How long have they been here?'

Dolly shrugged. 'They were out on the doorstep when I arrived. They've all been interviewed at the cop shop and Ruby's fixing cuppas for everyone.'

Pearl glanced towards her young waitress. 'And one for me too please,' she said, as she took off her jacket. Ruby smiled at her boss and put a selection of biscuits on a platter. Pearl braced herself. 'Okay,' she began. 'Let's see what they have to say.'

Seeing Pearl enter the restaurant from the kitchen, the allotment holders blurted several unintelligible questions in unison. Silence was restored only when Pearl held up a hand. Having taken control, she went on to explain:

'I'm sure you all have a lot to ask, but I have to tell you, I doubt I know more than you do.'

Madge glared at her. 'How can that be?' she said. 'You're meant to be a detective.'

'*And* you found the body,' said Michael.

'The police aren't allowing me to see to my hens,' complained Vanessa.

'Or my bees,' Ted grumbled.

'And *none* of us have been allowed anywhere near the allotment,' said Joe.

'But I . . . suppose that's usual in the circumstances, is it?' said Florence.

Pearl nodded. 'While the forensics officers are at work. And I hear you've all been interviewed?'

'Ruddy inquisition,' said Madge, turning to Dolly, who had come to sit beside her. 'I told them you drove me home after the meeting on Saturday.'

'So I did,' Dolly confirmed.

'And there I stayed,' said Madge, 'till I heard the news from Ted this morning.'

'I went down early today,' he said, 'had some weeding to do, but there was rozzer tape everywhere. White boiler suits padding around like something from a science-fiction film. I gave 'em my details but they wouldn't let me in.' He accepted a cup of tea from Ruby and a handful of Garibaldi biscuits.

'And they've told me I can't gain access to take care of my girls,' said Vanessa, sniffing into a handkerchief. Michael moved closer and laid a comforting hand on hers.

'I'm sure your hens will be taken good care of,' said Pearl, soothingly. 'The police will make sure of that.'

Madge piped up again. '*Will* they?' she asked, clearly unconvinced. 'They never even told Ted about the body, you know. He had to hear that from Dolly.'

'I had to let everyone know,' Dolly explained to Pearl, 'that the police would no doubt want to hear from us all. Especially after all those complaint letters.'

Vanessa appeared anxious. 'Do you think that might give them reason to suspect us?'

Pearl tried to calm her. 'I'm sure it's just a case of eliminating suspects. We were *all* at that meeting, including Franco, Marty and the Bessants, so we may well have been the last people to see Caroline alive.'

This idea appeared to settle in the minds of everyone until Dolly spoke:

'Apart from the murderer,' she said dolefully.

'True,' Pearl agreed. 'And I managed to speak to Franco yesterday,' she went on.

'How is he bearing up?' said Florence, with concern.

'Considering what's happened, not too badly,' said Pearl, 'but he'll need support – which the Bessants appear to be giving him at the moment.'

'And David Chappell?' asked Dolly.

'He's also given a statement,' said Pearl.

Madge gave a small grunt. 'He had the most to lose with those complaints.'

'Meaning what?' asked Vanessa, confused.

'Meaning,' said Ted, 'he may just have had more cause to take issue with that woman than any of us.'

'You're surely not suggesting he killed her, are you?' said Florence.

Madge tipped her head towards Ted. 'He's just thinking like a policeman.'

'Or a police*woman*,' said Dolly.

'That's right.' Ted nodded, savouring a Garibaldi. 'Some are superintendents these days.'

'Getting back to your point, Ted,' said Pearl, 'Caroline Lanzi *denied* having made any complaints.'

'Well, we've been through that, Pearl,' said Madge. 'She would deny it in the circumstances, wouldn't she?'

'That's right,' said Joe. 'And just because she did, it doesn't mean she was telling the truth.'

'She certainly had her own agenda,' said Michael. 'All the same,' he added quickly, 'she didn't deserve to die like that.'

'Is it true she was . . . stabbed?' asked Florence.

Pearl nodded.

Dolly explained: 'And her body was shoved into the composter.'

Madge considered this. 'One way of getting bigger pumpkins, I s'pose.'

Vanessa took a sharp breath. 'Madge, it's dreadful! And for you, Pearl, to have to find her like that.'

'If you ask me,' said Madge, 'there's something very fitting about her ending up there, seeing as she was so keen on us buying the blasted thing.'

'So what do we do now?' asked Ted.

'About the composter?' said Madge.

'About the police,' said Ted.

Before Pearl could reply, Michael spoke up. Leaning forward he said, in a hushed tone: 'I suggest we stick together and share information.'

'Good idea,' said Vanessa. 'We're all allotment holders, after all.'

'But we're forgetting someone,' said Joe. 'David?'

'I managed to talk to him,' said Pearl. 'And, as mentioned, he's also made a statement to the police. From what I can gather, and without any police confirmation, Caroline must have been murdered sometime after the meeting on Saturday and before I found her body on Sunday evening – just before eight p.m.'

Looks were exchanged until Dolly replied, 'As far as I know, we *all* went home after the meeting.'

Heads nodded. Pearl asked: 'Can everyone confirm that?'

'You mean with an alibi?' asked Joe.

'I can absolutely vouch for the fact that Joe came home with me,' said Florence. 'We were both busy at the cottage until very late last night.'

'I went to Vanessa's for a coffee after the meeting,' said Michael.

They shared a look, which prompted her to confide bashfully, 'And ... I went to Michael's last night for supper.'

'I drove Vanessa home after ten,' said Michael. 'We had some summer school ideas to discuss,' he offered, in a business-like tone.

'Mutual alibis,' said Pearl. 'Nothing more?'

Vanessa asked: 'What about you, Pearl?'

Deciding against explaining her run-in with David Chappell on the embankment path, she said only: 'I found the body, remember?' adding: 'And I do believe someone was at the allotment just before that.'

Ted dropped a Garibaldi biscuit before it reached his lips. 'The murderer, you mean?'

'Perhaps,' said Pearl.

A silence fell.

'And what about Marty?' said Michael, finally. 'He was at the meeting too.'

'I can't see that he could be implicated in any way,' said Pearl. 'As Caroline Lanzi's biggest fan he had absolutely no motive.'

'And,' said Dolly, 'she was probably his most important customer. Marty's always been far too impressed with material success.' She sniffed.

'Well,' said Michael, 'whatever the rest of us may have thought about Caroline, with her sense of privilege and entitlement, none of us would have wanted to see her lose her life – especially in such a grotesque way.'

'That's true,' Dolly agreed.

'I'm sure David Chappell feels the same,' said Pearl. 'I'm hoping I may have persuaded him to come to the fundraising event this evening.'

'For the carnival, you mean?' asked Florence.

Pearl nodded.

'Good idea,' said Dolly.

'Is it still going ahead?' asked Joe with some surprise.

'Life goes on,' said Madge.

'True enough,' said Ted, polishing off his last Garibaldi biscuit.

Pearl's phone sounded. Checking it, she saw it was a text from McGuire.

Can you meet me at the clock tower in Canterbury asap?

Pearl replied straight away.

I'll be there.

CHAPTER THIRTEEN

Once Pearl was confident that the brunch service was running smoothly at The Whitstable Pearl, she walked to the high street and took a bus into Canterbury. Parking in the city was always at a premium but the bus journey took only twenty minutes on a route that passed through the picturesque countryside of Pean Hill, Honey Hill and the village of Blean, with views of verdant fields stretching out on either side of the road, until cottage gardens appeared, their laburnum trees laden with luminous golden chains. The scenery always allowed Pearl some welcome distraction – a chance to take stock – until the eighteen-metre-high Westgate Towers came into view. The medieval gateway stood like a sentinel at the entrance to the great city of Canterbury.

A heat haze was shrouding the spires of the famous cathedral as Pearl alighted at the bus station and hurried to the venue McGuire had suggested – a clock tower, all that now remained of the church of St George the

Martyr in which the playwright Christopher Marlowe had been baptised. The tower featured a gilded clock projecting from the structure's wall, a historic landmark since the church had been demolished almost seventy years ago.

From the bus stop it was an easy stroll for Pearl on the main thoroughfare that would also have taken her to the cathedral where an old market place had once been sited, having long lost its former name of the Bullstake. It was a reminder of a more brutal time when cattle had been routinely tethered and baited with dogs to tenderise the meat before slaughter. Now the Butter Market provided a more innocuous title for the cobbled square that housed a fountain, coffee shops and bars as well as entrance to the cathedral for its nine hundred thousand annual visitors.

A few street-trader pitches were dotted along the main route to the clock tower, all that was now left of a popular city market that had recently been disbanded following an unpopular decision by local councillors. Local people bemoaned the loss, but not the departure of the councillors, who had gone on to lose their seats at the next election, including the council leader. Pearl threaded her way past shoppers and tourists, the latter easily identified as they posed for photographs by the clock tower, and caught sight of McGuire sitting at an al-fresco table in St George's Street, his crutches propped against his chair. She went quickly to him, bent down and kissed him. His smile was instantly reassuring.

'Are you okay?' he asked.

Pearl took the seat he had saved for her. 'Hale read me the Riot Act on failure to disclose information.'

'Only to be expected,' said McGuire, 'but don't let him bully you.'

'I won't,' she said, and ordered a coffee from a passing waitress. 'So, you were with Jackie Bates last night?' she asked, remembering McGuire's terse responses to her phone call.

'She's my best contact on this, Pearl,' he explained. '*And* she's no fan of Hale.'

'But a fan of yours?' Pearl let the question hang.

McGuire looked sidelong at her. 'If I'm not mistaken, those beautiful grey eyes of yours seem to be turning green.'

Pearl offered an arch smile. 'I would have liked to be with you myself last night.'

'Then you should give up finding dead bodies,' said McGuire, 'or at least allow the police to find their killers.'

The waitress brought Pearl's coffee, after which she settled closer to McGuire. 'So, what have you found out?'

He took out his iPad and began to scroll through it. 'Post-mortem results,' he began. 'You were right about the compost heat causing some anomalies.'

Pearl frowned. 'Body temperature usually remains stable between thirty minutes to an hour after death, but it can remain steady for up to five hours in some circumstances.'

McGuire nodded. 'If the body feels warm to the touch, and there's no rigor present, death's usually taken place within three hours.'

'If there's warmth *and* rigor,' said Pearl, 'it's likely to have taken place between three to eight hours earlier.'

McGuire agreed.

Pearl went on: 'Caroline's body was definitely warm, with no rigor, but we don't know how far that was affected by the composter.'

McGuire looked at her. 'From what I've found out, it appears she hadn't been dead for very long.'

'Cause of death?'

'Stab wounds.'

'Murder weapon?'

'An identified garden spading fork.'

'Forensics?'

'Footprints on local soil but considering the usual allotment foot traffic – *and* the number of allotment holders – nothing conclusive. Similarly with that spading fork, which had common use by you all.'

'What about eyewitness reports?'

McGuire shook his head. 'The allotments are a fair distance from the main residential area so it's not surprising house-to-house enquiries yielded nothing of value . . . It does seem you were right about Caroline Lanzi having spent the night at her studio.'

'Oh?'

'Evidence was found of candles having been lit.'

Pearl thought about this. 'The studio has solar panels so she didn't need to use candles.'

'Perhaps she didn't want to draw attention to her being there.'

Pearl nodded. 'Yes. It's against the regulations to spend the night at the allotment.'

'So,' said McGuire, 'it's possible she made her way there after the argument with her husband, decided to stay away from Franco on Saturday night, then met her killer sometime before you found her body just before eight on Sunday evening. It's also possible he was still at the allotment when you arrived, Pearl. You said you felt as though you were being watched?'

Pearl met McGuire's gaze. 'It's also possible that "he" was a "she". A woman could have murdered Caroline. That spading fork isn't too heavy,' she went on. 'The blades are incredibly sharp and presumably one blow would have been enough to dispatch her.'

McGuire nodded slowly.

Pearl continued, 'And the force could certainly have tipped her body back into the composter.'

McGuire remembered something. 'You're forgetting the body was *beneath* the compost.'

'Of course . . .' said Pearl, trailing off. 'And that means some of the compost must have been dumped out . . .'

'. . . in order to accommodate the body,' concluded McGuire.

'Then it was rearranged on top,' said Pearl, staring at him. 'I suppose the crime could have been premeditated after all.' She paused. 'But how could the killer have been sure she would be there?'

McGuire considered this. 'Franco could easily have assumed she would go there.'

'Yes,' said Pearl, 'and it's possible this wasn't the first time she'd spent the night there.'

'Equally,' said McGuire, 'David Chappell could have followed her. We know he'd been spying on the house.'

Pearl shook her head. 'But I told you, I saw him heading towards West Beach after the meeting.'

'And I told *you*, Pearl, that he had plenty of time to head back and realise Caroline was there. He could easily have come up with a plan, spied on her at the allotment, then killed her the next evening.'

Another thought came to Pearl's mind. 'It's also possible that one of the other allotment holders went there. They could have discovered her, then lied to the police, and me, about their movements. But I just can't imagine any of them murdering Caroline. Vanessa wouldn't say boo to a goose, Michael's a very reasonable man and a respected teacher. Joe and Florence are an incredibly kind and gentle couple, and Ted had his eightieth birthday not long ago.' She sipped her coffee.

'Is he strong?' asked McGuire.

'Yes,' said Pearl. 'He gardens most days and tends his bees . . .'

'What about the others – the ones who didn't receive a complaint?'

'Well . . .' Pearl began haltingly, then turned to McGuire and confided: 'I did happen to see Natasha Bessant talking to Franco on Sunday morning.'

'And?'

'And they both looked stressed, anxious – particularly Franco. But he did tell me later that day that he'd met Natasha to ask if she'd seen or heard from Caroline.'

McGuire turned towards the old clock tower as he ruminated on this. 'Or they could've been planning something. She could have helped him – as an accomplice?' He turned back to Pearl.

'But why?'

'Why else?' said McGuire. 'The two great motives for murder – love and money.'

Pearl reflected on this. McGuire was right, of course. 'It's quite possible,' she began, 'that Natasha's in love with Franco. He's an attractive man, after all, and her husband, Victor, seems to treat her like one of his beautiful artworks – another possession.' She thought for a moment. 'Franco also told me that Caroline was selling her company. The proceeds could certainly finance a new life for him . . . and Natasha.'

'Who else does that leave?' asked McGuire.

'We have to discount Marty.'

'Ah,' said McGuire. 'Your old flame!'

'Never!'

'Suitor.'

'*Would-be* suitor,' said Pearl. 'But he gave up long ago.'

'Some men never give up, Pearl. They like the chase.'

Pearl eyed him. 'And once the chase is over,' she said softly, 'and the prey is caught . . . That's it?'

'For some,' said McGuire, 'but not all.' He winked.

'Glad to hear it,' said Pearl, smiling now, before she remembered. 'There's still someone else . . .' Her smile was fading. 'Madge.'

'The woman with the pond?'

Pearl nodded. 'But she's one of Mum's oldest friends.'

'How old?'

'Old enough not to be a person of interest in this crime.'

McGuire raised an eyebrow.

'No. Madge is over seventy and, yes, she's still fit and strong, but the idea of her dispatching Caroline Lanzi and covering the body with heavy compost before hot-footing it up the embankment as soon as I arrived is very hard for me to imagine.'

'But it's possible,' said McGuire.

Pearl took a deep breath and pondered. 'Yes,' she conceded. 'It's possible.'

A moment passed before Pearl's phone sounded. She took it from her pocket and registered the caller. 'It's Mum.'

'I need you,' said Dolly, bluntly.

'What's wrong?'

'We've got a party of DFLs in, eating us out of oysters and drinking us out of Prosecco. I need to get home and check the glaze on that platter I'm donating for the carnival auction tonight. Whatever you're doing with McGuire, leave it till later, will you?'

As Dolly rang off, McGuire asked: 'What was that all about?'

Pearl gave a sudden smile. 'How about I buy you an Oyster Stout at the Neptune later?'

CHAPTER FOURTEEN

The Old Neptune, or the 'Neppy' as it was affectionately known by local people, was the only pub in Whitstable that stood on the beach. It had done so for centuries and in defiance of the elements, which had threatened its existence in a great storm in 1883. The entire structure had later been swept away in a devastating tidal surge, which had engulfed the pub and most of the town, but with the spirit of indefatigability that was characteristic of Whitstable, the Old Neptune had risen once more, refashioned from the timber reclaimed from its original construction. It continued to welcome the summer visitors, who flocked to its outside tables, and the locals who sought company, music and quiz nights in the long cold winters during which the north-easterly gales seemed to blow in directly from the Norwegian coast. This evening, the Neppy was packed for a special event: the donation of items for an upcoming auction to raise funds for the local carnival, due to take place on the first weekend of August.

Landlord Darrell Winton had set up an area in the public bar to display items that had already been donated, including scented candles, toiletries, an air-fryer and a set of framed photographs that featured the Old Neptune captured throughout the changing seasons. Pearl and Dolly had been wise enough to reserve a table, at which Madge Tolliday and Ted Rowden were also sitting, while Joe and Florence occupied another with Michael and Vanessa.

The bar, with its sloping floor, on which customers appeared either giants or Lilliputians, depending on where they stood, was packed with a sea of local residents through which Marty Smith suddenly appeared. He scanned the room and, on seeing Pearl, made a beeline for her, squeezing himself onto a vacant chair between her and Dolly without waiting for an invitation to do so.

'I have to say,' he began in a hushed tone, 'I'm surprised this is still happening – all things considered.'

'The carnival's going ahead,' said Pearl.

'And it needs funding,' said Dolly.

'Well, I s'pose you're right,' said Marty, glancing around the packed pub. 'Life goes on, and all that, but it wouldn't have hurt to defer this, if you ask me.'

'No one *did* ask you,' said Madge Tolliday, chomping a crisp. She gave Marty a knowing look. 'And I hope you're here to donate something, not just to gossip.'

Marty stiffened. 'I certainly am, Madge. As it happens, I'm here to pledge a Cornucopia fruit hamper,' he said proudly. 'How about you, Pearl?'

'A token,' she replied. 'A meal for two at The Whitstable Pearl.'

'*And* a bottle of wine,' added Dolly. 'I'm also throwing in one of my oyster platters.'

'Hopefully not throwing,' said Ted, with a smile, as he reached for his pint of beer.

'Very nice,' Marty commented. 'And what about you, my old friend?'

'Not so much of the "old",' said Ted, then answered Marty's question. 'Honey,' he said, and sipped his beer.

'Four jars,' said Madge, 'in a presentation box for which I've provided the ribbon.'

Ted smiled and Madge crowed: '*I'm* giving a mug commemorating King Edward the Eighth's coronation.'

'George the Sixth,' said Ted.

'You sure?' said Madge.

Dolly leaned towards her. 'Edward was the one that abdicated, remember?'

Puzzled, Madge looked to Ted for confirmation, but before he could reply, pub landlord Darrell had taken charge of a microphone to thank his customers for coming along and explained that the carnival's treasurer, Christopher James, would say a few words. A round of applause went up as an earnest-looking man in his early sixties took the microphone from Darrell to address the pub's customers.

'It means a lot to the carnival committee,' Christopher James began, 'to see so many of you here tonight. You'll know that a new committee took over the carnival only two years ago and we need funds urgently, for insurance purposes, but also to make sure everything goes well on the day so that we raise even more for local charities. We've already had quite a few pledges but any more will be gratefully received this evening.'

A round of applause quickly followed. A hand went up from the next table as Joe Fuller called: 'I'll pledge one of my wood carvings.' To further applause, he produced an A4-size photograph of his work, handing it to Darrell who placed it in pride of place on the display. Pearl was next with her token, followed swiftly by Marty, who made sure he let everyone know that he was offering a 'de luxe' Cornucopia fruit hamper, nothing mundane.

Also on the next table, Vanessa raised her hand. 'Don't tell me,' Marty sniggered, '*coq au vin*?'

Unamused, Vanessa ignored Marty while Michael called, 'I'd like to donate a set of wind chimes – all the way from China.'

Marty whispered to Pearl and Dolly: 'He's seen sense at last.'

'Sense?' asked Dolly.

'Well,' Marty continued, 'he's already had one complaint from the council about them.'

'A complaint *to* the council,' Dolly clarified.

'*From* Caroline Lanzi,' said Madge.

Marty raised a wagging finger. 'Now now, Madge,' he said, 'you're quite wrong there, because I was at the meeting when Mrs Lanzi denied making *any* complaints to *anyone*.'

'Yes,' said Madge, 'we all know what she *said*.' She gave Marty a grim look. 'You wouldn't be impugning the poor woman's honesty, would you, Madge? Surely not after what's happened – and especially since Mrs Lanzi is no longer here to defend herself.'

Ted nodded. 'He's right there, Madge, but if Mrs L didn't make the complaints, then who did?'

He looked at Marty, who saw that all eyes were now on him. He spluttered. 'Well, you—' Breaking off, Marty began again. 'You surely don't think *I* put in any complaints? Not my style!' he insisted. 'If I had anything to say about any one of you, I'd have said it to your face.'

'Yes,' said Pearl. 'I believe that's true – which means we're still none the wiser as to who *did* complain.'

As everyone paused to consider this, a voice called in the background: 'A painting from my gallery!'

Heads turned towards Victor Bessant, standing at the bar with Natasha. He went on to explain: 'It's worth at least a thousand pounds. *Raging Sea* by artist Trevor March.'

A loud murmur went around the room. 'My goodness!' said Dolly. 'If that's the reserve price it'll be easily reached at the auction. Trevor's work goes for a fortune these days.'

'But it's Victor who's making the pledge,' said Pearl, thoughtfully, 'which means he must have bought it from the artist to donate it.'

Dolly nodded. 'You're right, Pearl. So Victor won't have needed to pay his own outrageous commission. I'll bet he's also haggled Trevor down by telling him it's all for a good cause.'

Marty pulled a face. 'Why d'you always have to be so suspicious, Dolly? Mr Bessant doesn't need to donate anything.'

Ted sipped his beer again. 'He does if he's after some goodwill from this town.'

Before Marty could respond, the pub's door opened and McGuire suddenly appeared. Seeing Pearl at the table, he smiled and used his crutches to get across to her. Dolly greeted him first. 'Evening, Mike,' she said, no longer using her former nickname for McGuire, 'Flat Foot' – a public sign that she had accepted his relationship with Pearl and warmed to him. Pearl got quickly to her feet to greet him, then turned immediately to Marty.

'What?' Marty asked, feigning innocence, glass in hand.

'Your seat,' said Pearl. 'I was saving it.' She tipped her head to McGuire and Marty eyed his crutches, exhaling loudly in frustration as he finally got the message and stood up. As soon as Marty moved off, McGuire took his seat. 'Have I missed much?'

Madge leaned across to him. 'What're you donating?'

Confused, McGuire turned to Pearl but Ted moved closer to Madge to explain to her: 'That's Pearl's fella,' he said, 'the detective.'

Madge got the message but turned again to McGuire. 'Two tickets for the Policemen's Ball wouldn't go amiss.'

Ted shook his head. 'I don't think policemen have balls any more.'

Dolly smirked as more applause rang out – this time for the offer of a two-night stay at a local hotel.

McGuire saw Pearl's smile fade. 'What is it?' he asked.

'The Marine Hotel,' she said, her memory suitably jogged. 'It's up at Marine Parade in Tankerton. That was where David Chappell's wife, Cindy, was working when she got together with Russ Parker. David told me so the other night.' She picked up her drink. 'He also said he'd try to pop in here this evening. I hope he does because he needs to get back into the community and out of that bungalow of his.'

Dolly leaned in to her and said softly: 'It looks like he's taken your advice, Pearl.' She nodded to where David Chappell now stood by the pub's main window, which faced straight out to sea. Pearl noted immediately that he looked strained and was nursing a highball of amber liquid, which she instantly assumed must be whisky. As more offers came in for the auction, Pearl turned to McGuire. 'Let me get you an Oyster Stout.'

McGuire smiled and Pearl got up to head to the bar.

After she'd ordered the beer, Pearl managed to catch David Chappell's eye. He offered a tense smile and strolled across to her. 'Good to see you here.' She pointed to his glass. 'Can I get you another?'

'No, thanks. It's only apple juice.' He looked down at it, then saw that she was staring at him. 'Taste it, if you don't believe me.' He offered the glass.

'I believe you,' she said, 'and I'm glad you came. I know it's not easy.'

David gave a nod and cast a look around the crowded room, then heaved a heavy sigh. 'It's not easy, but you were right,' he said. 'I need to try to move on. I've known it all along but it's easier said than done.'

'Yes,' Pearl agreed. 'But hopefully things will get better for you.'

Across the room McGuire was engaged in conversation with Dolly, but as though he'd sensed her eyes on him, he looked up, met Pearl's gaze and smiled again, before continuing to listen to Dolly. In the next moment, she found herself focusing on him, remembering that she had needed no man while she had been bringing up Charlie because her son had been the only man in her life. She had become totally absorbed in his upbringing because her love for him was so strong. It remained undiminished, but on reaching forty she had felt as if she was entering a new era, the second act of a play in which she was a character, unsure of her role until McGuire had stepped onto her stage.

From time to time, Pearl tried to imagine life without him – but she couldn't. At one time David and Cindy must have felt the same way about each other, though it was clear their relationship had failed. Why? Because Cindy had fallen for Russ Parker? Or had the marriage soured before that? Pearl now found herself wondering whether David's drinking had begun on losing his wife, or was it the reason she had left him? Pearl paid for

McGuire's beer as David asked: 'What happened to your friend?' He nodded across to McGuire. 'He's a police officer, isn't he?'

'Sports injury. He wasn't seeing off any criminals. And he's not on the murder case, if that's what you're thinking.'

'Have they . . . got any leads?' David asked.

Pearl shrugged. 'Not that I know of. Yet. But I'm sure the killer will be found.'

'How can you be so confident?'

'A murder like that,' Pearl began, 'an attack at an allotment? It still seems to me to have been opportunistic. And with no time to plan, the killer is bound to have made some mistakes, left a trace.' David eyed her. Pearl explained. 'One of the most important things I learned from my police training was that every contact leaves a trace. That means a criminal is sure to leave something at the scene of the crime. It's a basic principle of forensic science and it's only ever a matter of time before that trace is found.'

David Chappell seemed to consider this very carefully before he nodded in agreement. 'I hope so,' he said.

Applause rang out once more as someone made a donation. Pearl smiled. 'Care to join us?' she asked, picking up McGuire's drink. David thanked her, and they set off for Pearl's table.

As they did so, a loud voice yelled across the room: 'A big bottle of bubbly!'

Pearl stopped, recognising the familiar gravelly tone. David Chappell did the same, and both turned. Two people had entered the pub: a suntanned Russ Parker stood with his arm around Cindy Chappell, holding aloft a magnum of champagne and grinning at the applause that greeted his donation.

In that moment, Cindy appeared to Pearl like a Pre-Raphaelite heroine, with long ember-red curls falling almost to her waist as she kissed Russ's cheek. He came forward and set the magnum on the display table. Cindy hung back as her eyes locked with her husband's. David Chappell had turned to stone. Customers began to engage Russ in conversation, and as he leaned forward to hear their comments, Pearl saw that Cindy appeared to be steeling herself to pass her husband on her way to Russ. As she did so, David reached out and grabbed her arm.

'David,' said Pearl, sharply, in an effort to restrain him, but he maintained his hold on Cindy, his eyes still fixed on her.

'What are you doing here?' he demanded, in a hushed whisper.

'What do you mean?' Cindy asked. 'This is my town as well as yours.'

'You disappeared,' he said. 'You left me – for him!' He jerked his head towards Russ, who had caught sight of what was happening and strode quickly across.

'Take your hands off her,' he ordered.

David ignored him, his eyes remaining on Cindy as he reminded her: 'You're still my wife.'

'More's the pity,' said Russ. 'And I'm not going to tell you twice,' he warned, stepping closer. 'Let go of her.'

David's gaze dropped to his hand, which was still gripping Cindy's arm. As if coming out of a dream, he loosened his grasp and allowed Cindy to free herself.

'Don't you go near her again,' Russ ordered, putting his arm around Cindy to steer her away. Pearl found herself taking a deep breath, relieved the incident was over, until David whirled round and grabbed Russ's shoulder, spinning his rival to plant a punch on him. But before he could do so, something came down between the two men, landing with a bang on a table. McGuire was suddenly there – using one of his crutches as a barrier to separate them.

'That's enough,' he ordered.

The pair still held one another's eyes as Russ spoke, still seething with anger. 'You're a madman, you know that?' He indicated David to McGuire and Pearl. 'This man's dangerous, you hear?'

Pearl saw that David was trying his best to control himself, a muscle clenching in his jaw, before he turned on his heels and pushed his way through the crowded pub to the door. Once it had slammed after him, Pearl noticed his glass, dumped on the table before her. She picked it up and sniffed the contents, taken aback by the strong scent of whisky.

CHAPTER FIFTEEN

'What on earth are Russ and Cindy doing back in town?' Pearl was in her restaurant kitchen the next day, preparing Mignonette sauce using chopped shallots, white wine, sugar and black pepper.

'Well,' mused Dolly, 'as Cindy quite rightly said, this *is* their home.'

'Except Cindy walked out on hers,' said Pearl, 'and Russ sold his when they disappeared off together to Marbella.'

'Yes,' Dolly agreed. 'Everyone thought they were planning to live in Spain.' She frowned. 'So, why come back now?'

'That's something I aim to find out,' Pearl told her.

Dolly observed Pearl as she set the Mignonette sauce in the middle of one of her own platters, with a dozen Pacific rock oysters. 'Some would say that's not your business, Pearl.'

Pearl handed the order of oysters to Ruby, waiting until the waitress had disappeared into the restaurant to set Dolly straight. 'While David remains a suspect in Caroline's murder it's very much my business. I made a promise to Franco that I would find his wife's killer, remember?'

Dolly gave her a sidelong look. 'And while you're doing that he gets access to any information you might uncover?' She continued, leaning closer: 'If he had anything to do with his wife's murder—'

Pearl broke in: 'I know. He remains one step ahead while he's hiring me to investigate. He also has a very good motive – the money from the sale of the business.'

'And a possible relationship with Natasha?' said Dolly.

Pearl demurred. 'I don't know if I was ever right about that,' she said, troubled. 'Franco and Natasha are attractive individuals so it looks as if they may well be more suited to one another than to their partners, for one reason or another . . .' She trailed off.

'Franco was certainly younger than his wife,' said Dolly. 'But age should never stop two people loving one another.'

'And you're right that Natasha seems to be under Victor's thumb.'

'"Seems" may be the operative word,' said Dolly. 'It's true none of us can know what goes on behind closed doors.' She conceded: 'But your instincts are usually spot on.'

'Doesn't mean I can't make mistakes.'

'Yes, but it was a good idea of yours to invite Mike to the Neppy last night – *and* his crutches.'

Pearl smiled. 'He's been moping around since the accident. And, like David Chappell, he needs to get out and about . . . Plus I miss him.'

Dolly raised an eyebrow. 'So, now you've got him involved in this case. Clever.'

Pearl moved to the sink and washed her hands. 'He's following up some leads for me today – and it's not long until that cast comes off.'

'And then?' asked Dolly.

'Maybe it'll be time for us to move forward.'

Dolly straightened. 'Am I going to need to buy a hat?' she asked. 'For the wedding?'

'Watch this space,' said Pearl, enigmatically. 'Until then, I've got some leads I want to follow up on myself.'

Before Dolly could respond, Pearl's phone rang. She wiped her hands on her apron, then listened, finally thanking the caller.

'Well?' asked Dolly.

'That was Audrey,' said Pearl. 'The receptionist at the Marine? I had an idea Cindy and Russ might be staying there. Turns out I was right. Apparently Cindy's just picked up a beach picnic from the chef. Can you manage here for a while?'

Dolly shrugged. 'If I have to.'

'Good,' said Pearl, taking off her apron. 'I'm in the mood for some sea air.'

*

Less than ten minutes later, Pearl was parking her Fiat on Marine Parade – a long coastal road in the neighbouring town of Tankerton on which the Marine Hotel stood, looking straight out to sea. It was high tide, the estuary waters reflecting the deep blue sky above with no sign of the Street of Stones – the mile-long stretch of shingle that became visible with the lowering tide. No one knew for sure how the mysterious spit had sprung into existence: some believed it to be the remains of a Roman road built on land that had later been surrendered to the sea; others claimed it had once been an ancient landing stage for vessels. It also served as a clear marker for free fishing waters but always remained obscured at high tide, reappearing only when the waters retreated, like a sharp golden arrow pointing towards the horizon.

Pearl noted that paddle-boarders and canoeists were out in force but closer to the shore a few swimmers were enjoying a calm sea. Pearl slipped on a sunhat and headed down a path on a grassy embankment known locally as the Slopes, on which Edwardian holidaymakers had promenaded. The area of Tankerton Slopes was now mainly home to rows of brightly painted beach huts that were changing hands for sums that would have bought a local house only a couple of decades ago.

Approaching the pebbled shore, Pearl caught sight of a few families keeping a watchful eye on young children in the shallows. One figure sat alone on the beach, unmistakable to Pearl with her long fiery curls. Cindy Chappell wore a scarlet swimsuit and dark glasses as she stared out to sea, her eyes trained on a swimmer now wading towards the shore. Russ Parker's bronzed body glistened in the sunlight as he pushed his coal-black hair back from his forehead and smiled. Cindy tossed a towel to him, then watched as he threw it onto the beach and fell onto it. She leaned forward and kissed him, slowly, as though savouring every moment. Pearl was reminded of a time more than twenty years ago when she, too, had sat on the same spot with a young man called Carl, during a summer that had changed the course of her life.

Pearl's first love had been powerful. It had left its mark on her heart but also on her life in the form of Charlie. Carl, a young Australian, had been there for the summer, passing through and working in a local bar until he had saved enough money to head off to the Far East. Harbouring his own ambitions to be an artist, he didn't want to be tied down – though he did want Pearl, who was due to start her new job that autumn. Leaving with Carl would have meant abandoning her future, her family, her home, her life, which she had been unable to do – especially on finding she was pregnant. Instead, Pearl had clung to an old maxim of Dolly's: 'if you love something, then set it free. If it comes back it's yours. If it doesn't, it never was.'

Ultimately, Carl had proved himself to be the free spirit Pearl had always known him to be. He had disappeared from her life leaving her to transfer all her love to Charlie, aware that the only thing her son had ever missed out on was a father. Life had moved on, and two decades later, McGuire had filled the vacant space in Pearl's heart. A different relationship. A different bond between two people who were both aware of the heavy price that could be paid for love.

Pearl refocused on the two figures on the beach before she took a step forward to join them.

'Pearl.' Cindy spoke first, her hand shielding her eyes against the sunlight. 'Aren't you meant to be at the restaurant?'

Pearl shook her head. 'Mum's in charge,' she explained. 'I'll be back soon.' She offered a smile.

'Sit down,' said Russ, an invitation for her to join them.

Pearl did so, taking off her hat and staring out to sea. 'I was surprised to see you both last night. Have you been back long?'

Russ and Cindy exchanged a look. 'A few days now,' said Russ.

'But we were in Margate,' Cindy explained. 'Thought we'd keep out of Dave's way, but then . . .'

As she trailed off, Russ continued: 'We thought why should we? So we booked into the Marine on Monday afternoon, then heard there was a bit of a do on at the Neppy last night, and went along.'

Cindy sighed. 'We didn't expect to see Dave there, Pearl. He's never been one for pubs.'

Russ gave a dark look. 'Though that's not to say he hasn't got a liking for the drink.' He lay back on the beach.

'Is that true?' asked Pearl.

Cindy nodded, then poured sun lotion onto her hands. For a few moments, she stroked Russ's toned biceps. "Fraid so, Pearl. Scotch. Dave's got a problem but he won't admit it. It got worse as time went on. All he ever did was work and drink.' She looked pained. Russ quickly laid his hand on hers and she continued. 'To tell you the truth, Pearl, I was glad to get away from him. He became so unpredictable. You saw how he was last night. That temper of his . . .'

Russ gently stroked her forearm.

'Once the red mist descends you don't want to be around him.' Cindy shook her head. 'He'd always be sorry afterwards, but he'd never get help. I couldn't have stayed with him any longer. Meeting Russ was the best thing that could have happened to me.'

Pearl saw Russ give her a wink. Cindy smiled and returned it. 'And what now?' asked Pearl.

'What d'you mean?' asked Russ.

'Well, you're back and . . . considering what happened last night—'

Cindy faced Pearl. '"Considering" nothing,' she said firmly. 'Dave and I are separated. I've got a new life now with Russ – all I need to do is get divorced.'

'And what if "Dave" doesn't want to?' wondered Pearl.

Russ propped himself on an elbow. 'It doesn't matter if he wants to or not. He's going to have to, Pearl. Because we need to move on.'

Pearl looked between them. 'Spain?'

'No, we won't be going back now,' said Russ. 'It was good while it lasted but things didn't pan out. I need to get back to work here, and we can't afford to live in a hotel for ever.'

Cindy explained: 'The Marine's given us a good deal while Russ does some work in their conservatory but he'll need more soon. Do you think you could put the word out that he's back? Here . . .' She reached into her bag and produced a handful of flyers, advertising Russ Parker's skills as a roofer and scaffolder, then handed them to Pearl.

'If you could possibly see your way to putting some of those in the restaurant, and Dolly's shop,' said Russ, 'it'd be much appreciated.'

'Okay,' said Pearl.

Cindy went on: 'We'll get straight soon. I'm owed half the value of the bungalow. Dave and I got the mortgage together.'

'Of course,' said Pearl.

Cindy gestured to her bag. 'We should have this picnic before it gets too hot, Russ.'

'Care to join us?' asked Russ.

'Thanks,' said Pearl, 'but I'd better get back to the restaurant.' She got to her feet and slipped on her sun-hat. 'Have the police been in touch?'

'Police?' echoed Cindy. 'You mean about that murder at the allotment?'

Russ put on a T-shirt. 'We were up in the Marine's bar the night it happened.'

'Yes,' said Cindy. 'We'd just arrived from Margate. Had an early supper there and got involved with a few regulars in the bar till closing time.'

'Heard it was some DFL,' said Russ. 'Why would the police want to talk to us?'

'Well,' said Pearl, turning to Cindy, 'presumably your name is down on the licence for the allotment plot.'

Cindy shook her head. 'No. That was something Dave did on his own. I knew it would be a mistake. A stupid idea, because he was bound to get bored with it. It was nothing to do with me.'

Pearl nodded. 'Well, I'll leave you to your picnic.' She turned back to them suddenly. 'Come to the restaurant soon,' she said. 'Now that you're back. I'd like to treat you both to dinner.'

Cindy and Russ seemed equally delighted at the thought. 'Thanks, Pearl,' said Cindy.

'Try keeping us away,' said Russ, with a wink.

CHAPTER SIXTEEN

'I can't believe we were talking about Caroline only the other day and now . . .' Councillor Peter Radcliffe was unusually lost for words. He closed his eyes momentarily, then opened them and beckoned Pearl to follow him into a room off the hallway in the Old Captain's House. 'Best we talk in my office,' he explained. 'Hilary's having a home massage.'

Pearl was well aware that Radcliffe's wife was an attractive woman who spent a small fortune on keeping herself so, with regular beauty treatments and a hairdressing bill to match Pearl's mortgage. As Radcliffe indicated that she should take a seat opposite his own at an antique desk, Pearl glanced around, noting photos in ostentatious frames – one in pride of place showing Radcliffe and Hilary with the current Mayor of Canterbury, a stout woman with a blue rinse wearing ceremonial robes, a tricorn hat decorated with ostrich feathers and what looked to Pearl like a ton of gold bullion around her neck.

Positioned behind Radcliffe, in the kind of conspicuous arrangement only someone of his vanity might find appropriate, several shelves were lined with trophies, mostly for cricket, a few for golf and some for outdoor bowls, alongside framed certificates and accolades for the councillor's municipal achievements. As Pearl sat down, she imagined Radcliffe might be regretting that it was now too late for any evidence of his relationship with Caroline Lanzi to be added to the same shelves. He collected his thoughts, and adjusted the position of his toupee. 'You said in your text that you needed my help?'

'Yes,' said Pearl. 'I mentioned that I'd like a few words with you, if you don't mind. About the complaints?'

A frown passed across Radcliffe's brow, as though he was trying to compute something. 'Oh, yes, of course,' he replied. 'You asked if I could find out who had lodged them.'

'And I wouldn't ask if it wasn't important,' said Pearl.

'I don't see how,' said Radcliffe, appearing equally confused and nettled by Pearl's comment. 'The council operates a strict policy on keeping such information confidential for obvious reasons.'

'You mean . . . to avoid any potential repercussions on complainants?'

'Precisely,' said Radcliffe. 'However,' he continued, 'in the circumstances that doesn't apply in this case.'

'Because Caroline Lanzi's now dead?'

Radcliffe fixed Pearl with a hard look. 'Because the complainant was un-named.'

Pearl sat back in her chair as she processed this news, while Radcliffe reached into his desk drawer and pulled out a buff-coloured folder. 'You mean the complaints were all made anonymously?'

'That's right,' said Radcliffe, opening his folder and slipping on a pair of glasses. 'I made enquiries and . . .' He checked the paperwork before he went on. 'The complaints were submitted as typewritten letters sent by mail to the relevant department detailing the breaches committed by each allotment holder.'

'No email address then,' said Pearl, 'and no signature, name or address on any of them?'

'Nothing.' He closed the folder.

'What about the envelopes they arrived in?' asked Pearl. 'A postmark could have given some details of the area in which they were posted.'

'They were all destroyed on receipt,' he said. 'That's usual council procedure.'

'And the letters themselves?' asked Pearl, hopefully.

'Scanned for council records. It's much easier to keep digital records these days than paper.'

Pearl was crestfallen. Radcliffe now raised the folder in his hand. 'It's all strictly confidential, of course, but I did personally check on that,' he went on. 'As you know, I held Mrs Lanzi in very high esteem.' He paused before leaning forward to announce, 'I sincerely hope you find her killer.'

*

Still feeling disappointed as she left the Old Captain's House, Pearl was heading along Harbour Street when she passed The Front and noticed that the gallery now featured some striking new work in its window. She took a few moments to admire the three creatures carved in wood, then saw Joe Fuller and Florence Brightling inside with Victor Bessant. She decided to join them.

On seeing Pearl enter, Florence's face lit up. 'Pearl!'

'I've just seen the new window display,' Pearl explained, pointing at it. 'It's amazing.'

'I agree,' said Victor. 'The oil seascape has been delivered to the carnival committee, all ready for the auction, and we're delighted to have some of Joe's work in its place.' He moved to the window as the others followed. 'Care to tell Pearl all about it, Joe?'

Joe Fuller smiled, clearly happy to do so. 'I worked the large bison piece from spalted beech.'

'Spalted?' said Pearl.

Joe nodded. 'It's a term used to describe what happens after fungi grow on dead or fallen trees. They colonise the timber and travel up the cells leaving a distinct pattern on the wood. Lots of timbers can "spalt" but it's most common with beech. It was quite a few years before I could use this. It was so incredibly fragile I had to file most of it, rather than carving.'

Victor was clearly impressed. 'And it's been inspired by primitive art. Early cave paintings?'

'Exactly right,' said Joe, pleased and no doubt flattered, thought Pearl, by the gallery owner engaging with his work. He pointed to the second piece – a coiled snake. 'This python is carved from oak and based on a spiral theme I've been exploring.' Then he indicated the final piece: a series of intricate snail shells also worked from oak. 'And these rams' horns were carved from the off-cuts of larger pieces of work. They're freshwater snails, and a bit of an aquarium pest, but you also find them in garden ponds.'

Florence smiled proudly. 'Joe spotted some in Madge's pond at the allotment.'

'That's right,' Joe confirmed. 'And I'm glad I did. Good inspiration. They have the look of fossils about them, don't you think?'

'Yes,' Pearl agreed, fascinated by the complexity of Joe's work, 'rather like ammonites.' She turned her attention to the young artist. 'It's wonderful that your work is getting such good exposure.'

'Thanks to Mr Bessant,' said Florence.

'Victor,' he said. 'I'm always keen to exhibit good work – and support members of our local artists' community.'

'Well, I appreciate it,' Joe said sincerely, 'especially at the moment.'

'Yes,' said Florence, as she slipped an arm through Joe's. 'It's all very timely and such a relief for us.'

'That's the way the world goes round – or should. We help one another.' Victor bestowed a warm smile on Florence, which she returned coyly. Then he turned to Pearl. 'My wife will tell you,' he said, 'I was once an artist so I appreciate the struggle to get work into the public eye.'

Pearl glanced around the gallery. 'Is Natasha here?'

'With Franco,' said Victor. 'He's finding it very hard to deal with Caro's death.' He paused, suitably sombre. 'We all are.'

'Yes,' Pearl agreed.

An uncomfortable silence settled, broken by Florence. 'Well,' she said, 'we really should be going. Floss will be waiting.'

'Floss?' asked Pearl.

Florence explained: 'She's our new kitten. Only eight weeks old so I don't like to leave her alone for too long.'

With the sudden change of mood, Pearl also decided to take her leave when a thought came to her. Looking again at Joe's carvings, she asked: 'Wasn't all this work stored at the allotment?'

'That's right. After I lost my workshop.'

'So how did it get here today?'

'The police have finished their forensic enquiries,' said Florence. 'We were all allowed back on the plots this morning. Didn't you know?'

Pearl took a moment to assimilate this. 'No, I didn't,' she replied, taken aback. 'Thanks for telling me.'

CHAPTER SEVENTEEN

A short while after leaving Victor Bessant's gallery, Pearl pushed open the rusting gate to the
allotment and was reminded of the last time she had
been here. She'd detoured from her journey to Canterbury to pick up McGuire so they could have a meal
together – a special meal that had gone uneaten due
to the discovery of Caroline Lanzi's dead body. It had
been a premature and ignominious end to a woman's
life, so much of which had been spent either promot-
ing the careers of her celebrity clients or trying to bury
any bad news that might have damaged them. From
recent online research Pearl had learned that Caroline's
own career had been filled with stellar social events – a
hectic schedule of opening-night invitations and inter-
national travel until, at what appeared to have been the
peak of her company's success, the businesswoman and
her attractive younger husband had decided to sell up
and purchase a property in a small north Kent town

that was most famous for the brown bivalve known as the native oyster.

For centuries, the prized mollusc had provided work and sustenance for Whitstable's inhabitants at a time when ship construction had dominated the town's shores and tall three-masted schooners had towered over the roofline of homes like Pearl's Seaspray Cottage. Centuries ago, more than a hundred master mariners had been listed in the town while the oyster trade had flourished. Nowadays, the old yawls were only to be seen during local regattas although one, known as the *Favourite*, sat moored for ever on the shingle bank alongside Pearl's home. Its bowsprit pointed like an accusing finger at a block of new-build apartments across the road. Whitstable's oyster tradition continued in the form of the town's annual festival, as well as on the menu of Pearl's restaurant, but fishing for the native oyster had almost disappeared once the farming of Pacific rock oysters had begun to take place on metal trestles on the foreshore.

The rock oyster had become so prolific that it was now considered an invasive species, having escaped local containment to spread along the Kent coast at such a rate that it threatened other sea life. Local fishermen talked of rock oysters weighing more than two kilos, monsters taking over the local marine ecology to such an extent that environmental groups were working hard with volunteers to destroy the species. They likened the farming of rock oysters for profit to growing Japanese knotweed in poly-tunnels. In other coastal areas, a similar programme of removal had been put in place, not least because the razor-sharp shells of the Pacific rock oysters, which sat vertically rather than horizontally on the sea bed, were sharp enough to penetrate the soles of rubber boots and injure the feet of sailors jumping out of their boats at low tide.

There were parallels between the threat from the rock oyster and the other non-native invasive species, the DFL, with the likes of the Lanzis and the Bessants supplanting locals by increasing the demand for Whitstable properties, thereby pushing up prices out of the range of most local families. Pearl's son, Charlie, had been forced out of town by the lack of affordable properties to rent instead a tiny student flat in Canterbury – a city filled with tourists, bars and chain stores in contrast to all he had grown up with in Whitstable. To Pearl's chagrin, he had become a 'city boy', when he wasn't in need of his old room at Pearl's. Now it had become clear that the expansion of the DFLs had spread to the local allotments, including Pearl's, with tragic consequences. Pearl thought back to the morning she had been startled by a cacophony beyond her own plot cabin, and her subsequent discovery of David Chappell, distressed but also furious on receipt of a notice from the council following a recent complaint. David had been convinced that the complainant had been Caroline Lanzi – a woman used to being in control, who had taken the reins and focused her own ambitions on the site. She had initially used her own plot and studio as a venue for social afternoons with the Bessants, then forced the purchase of a hot composter on all of the allotment holders. Ultimately it had become her tomb. Her most recent plan to form the Allotment Association would surely now go unrealised but Pearl found herself revisiting the question that remained lodged in her mind: could the mounting resentment of one of Pearl's fellow plot holders have provided sufficient motive for homicide?

On her way down towards the plots, she halted as she recalled Caroline Lanzi's lifeless eyes staring up at her . . . her features smeared with compost . . . a filthy hand decorated with a single diamond glinting in the fading sunlight. Diamonds were eternal. Not so Caroline Lanzi.

Pearl took a deep breath and tried to refocus her thoughts before moving on towards the Nolan plot. A breeze was blowing through the embankment trees and, apart from the absence of the composter and the familiar sound of Michael's Chinese wind chimes, it appeared just like any other summer's day at the allotment. The drone of Ted Rowden's bees hung on the warm air while frogs could be heard leaping in Madge Tolliday's pond. Birdsong filled the sky, uninterrupted by any human sounds, until Pearl heard the faint but unmistakable murmur of a woman weeping.

Following the sound, Pearl found herself at the chicken run, near which Vanessa, in tears, was being comforted by Michael and Madge. At a short distance, Ted Rowden stood thrusting a spade into a pile of soil, which he dropped into a small hole.

'What on earth's happened?' asked Pearl. Vanessa looked up but it was Madge who explained.

'There's been another murder,' she replied grimly.

As Pearl joined them, Michael qualified: 'Not exactly, Pearl. One of Vanessa's hens has died.'

'Poor Charity,' whimpered Vanessa, then blew her nose. 'She was already gone when I arrived, passed over the rainbow bridge. Pet heaven,' she explained. She gave a long sigh. 'She must have thought I'd deserted her. Perhaps she even assumed she'd be sent back to the battery farm.'

Seeing she was becoming increasingly upset, Michael spoke up. 'I think it's unlikely a chicken would be capable of that level of deduction. Their brains are really very small.'

Madge offered a firm opinion. 'No one can be sure what a chicken thinks till they've walked around in its shoes.'

Michael rolled his eyes at this, but Pearl moved closer to investigate. 'Was there any damage to the coop?' she asked.

Vanessa shook her head. 'None,' she said, 'and it wasn't a fox because Faith and Hope are unscathed and the whole run is secure.'

Pearl leaned in to see the two other hens strutting about, but before she could respond, Ted came across, having finished his digging and set down his spade. 'All done,' he said, taking off his gardening gloves. 'I dug it deep enough to fox the foxes.'

'You should have let me help you,' said Michael.

'Yes,' said Madge, 'digging chicken graves in this weather is hard.'

'Thirsty work,' said Ted, taking off a spotted kerchief from his neck and mopping his brow.

'Right,' said Madge. 'Let's go over to your hut, Ted, and have a glass of lemonade.'

'Good idea,' Michael said, offering a smile to Vanessa. 'You go with Madge and Ted while I talk to Pearl.'

Vanessa allowed Madge to steer her towards Ted's wartime Anderson shelter. Michael waited until they had entered it before turning to Pearl, his expression darkening. 'It really is insufferable,' he began, 'watching Vanessa so upset. She adored those hens, but since the murder, the police wouldn't allow her anywhere near them until today. Who knows if they were taken proper care of?'

Pearl nodded to the hens' run where Faith and Hope were relishing a dust bath in some soil. 'The other two look well,' she said. 'I'm sure the police would have followed procedure for animal welfare and made sure they were all taken good care of.'

Michael wasn't placated but wiped his face with his hand. '*None* of this would have happened if the Lanzis hadn't moved here!' He turned away in an effort to control his temper, then turned back to Pearl to explain calmly: 'Vanessa is a very sensitive and caring human being. Perhaps too sensitive.'

'What do you mean?'

'I mean,' said Michael, 'she's too sensitive for her own good. I've seen the way she takes care of the children at the nursery – as if they were her own.'

'I'm sure you feel the same about the kids you teach,' said Pearl.

He raked a hand through his hair. 'I wish I did,' he said, 'but teaching is a very stressful occupation, these days. We're set so many goals, have to achieve results, maintain standards. Coming to this allotment was part of my own way of coping.' He glanced around. 'On a day like this it's a little bit of Eden. Or it was before Caroline Lanzi arrived.' He took a deep breath. 'I won't lie, Pearl. I disliked the woman and all she stood for, profiting from self-interest. And then I look at Vanessa, how much she does with the children and the animals she cares for. She helps several animal charities, you know. In fact, she's just placed a kitten that needed rehoming with Florence.'

'So that's where it came from,' said Pearl. Michael looked at her and she explained. 'Florence happened to mention it. Floss?'

Michael gave a nod. 'It isn't fair that someone as kind as Vanessa should have to suffer losses herself, Pearl. You may say it was only a rescue hen but it was much more to Vanessa – and caring for those creatures is a sign of her humanity. She's been worrying ever since the council wrote to her about her hens – now this?'

Pearl remained silent, allowing him the space to conclude.

'It breaks my heart to see her so upset,' he said.

'I can understand that, Michael. And I do sympathise.'

She said nothing more as Michael set off in the direction of Ted's Anderson shelter to join the woman Pearl was now convinced he loved. With Victor Bessant's comment still fresh in her mind, she glanced back towards the rusting gate, feeling the need to check on two other people.

Instead of going home, Pearl decided to take the path that led to the rear of the Lanzis' house, having remembered that Natasha Bessant had gone to comfort Franco. The weather was sufficiently fine for Pearl to hope she might catch a glimpse of the pair in the garden.

After waiting for some dog walkers to move along the public path, she mounted a sloping ridge that allowed her to peer into the garden. Through the fence, she spotted Franco seated at a table by the swimming-pool, his head in his hands as Natasha moved closer to slip a comforting arm around his shoulders. It was impossible to hear what was being said but Pearl remained in place, in case the two might at some point move closer to the bottom of the garden to take in the sea view. After some time, Franco looked slowly up at Natasha and said a few words. Natasha pushed her hand gently through his silver hair. The pair seemed lost in one another's eyes, neither moving but instead frozen in time, like two figures in a photograph.

Pearl waited in considerable suspense to see what might happen next but her phone rang loudly in her pocket, its volume steadily increasing without her reply. She was forced to switch it off without registering who the caller was. Looking through the fence again, Pearl saw that Natasha was now staring in her direction. Was it possible she had heard Pearl's ringtone?

Taking no chances, Pearl stepped down from the ridge and hurried along the path to the lower embankment where she was sure she was concealed by some tall trees near the railway bridge. There, she caught her breath, took her phone from her pocket and switched it on again to find she had missed a call from McGuire. She dialled him back. He answered straight away. 'Pearl?'

'I'm sorry,' she replied. 'What is it?'

'I'm on my way to you right now,' McGuire said. 'Hale's going public with the murder tonight. He's recorded an appeal for the early-evening news.'

CHAPTER EIGHTEEN

An hour later, Pearl was sitting close to McGuire on the sofa in Seaspray Cottage. He glanced at her before switching on the TV with the remote. 'This is a mistake,' he said.

'How can you be so sure?'

'Because Caroline Lanzi had a public profile, as do many of her clients. Hale probably thinks he'll have one too after this but his officers will be wasting precious time, tripping over reporters from now on. And,' he went on, 'if word gets out that it was you who found the body, they'll be crawling all over the restaurant too.' He was clearly concerned. 'Maybe you should think about coming to stay with me.'

'In the man-cave?' said Pearl.

'I can tidy up.' McGuire smiled.

'Much as I'd love to spend more time with you,' said Pearl, 'I really need to be in Whitstable right now.'

'I know,' said McGuire, resigned, 'and if you hadn't been here this afternoon you might have missed seeing Franco and Natasha together.'

Pearl felt uneasy. 'I'm still not quite sure what it was I saw.'

McGuire picked up the Oyster Stout in front of him. 'Come on, Pearl. You surely know the signs by now.'

'Signs?'

'The look that passes between two people when they're . . .' He trailed off, holding Pearl's gaze, moving closer until his lips met hers in a sweet slow kiss. As they gently broke apart, his eyes still scanned her face. 'When this is all over . . .'

'Yes?'

'You and I are going to—' He stopped abruptly at the sound of the signature tune for the local TV news.

'Quick!' he ordered, searching for the remote, but Pearl found it first and switched up the volume as DI Hale appeared on screen. 'Ah, he's not alone,' noted McGuire, taking a sip of his beer.

'With Franco,' said Pearl, 'and DS Jackie Bates.' She turned to McGuire. 'She really is very attractive.'

McGuire gave an innocent shrug. 'Is she?' He gave a playful smile, which Pearl returned before he asked: 'You *are* recording this?'

'Of course.'

The newsreader finished an introduction, then handed over to 'Detective Inspector John Hale of Canterbury CID.'

'At least he's got a clean tie on,' said Pearl.

As if on cue, Hale straightened his tie, and appeared uncomfortable in the formal suit he was wearing. Then he explained that the murder of Mrs Caroline Lanzi had been a devastating event for the local community but especially for her husband Franco. 'Which is why we are mounting this appeal tonight for information,' Hale went on, 'particularly regarding any possible sighting of Mrs Lanzi in the vicinity of the allotments.'

A woman now appeared on the screen, walking across the allotment site.

'They're using a body double,' said McGuire.

'And she's wearing an outfit very similar to the one Caroline was wearing at our meeting on Sunday evening . . . taupe trousers and—'

'Tope?' said McGuire, clearly mystified.

'Taupe,' Pearl repeated. 'A greyish-brown colour. It's actually French for "mole".'

McGuire considered this. 'Sounds a lot more attractive than it does in English.'

He set down his Oyster Stout as Pearl studied what the body double on screen was wearing. 'Presumably Franco gave Hale those clothes,' she mused, thinking about the evening at the Lanzis' house.

McGuire picked up his glass and sipped his drink. 'It wouldn't be the same outfit Caroline had been wearing. That would have been saved as a forensic exhibit.'

Pearl realised something. 'But that *could* be something belonging to Natasha Bessant – she would have remembered what Caroline had been wearing that night.'

'Would she?' asked McGuire.

'She's a woman. We notice these things.' A thought occurred to her. 'You know, it's possible that's the reason I saw Natasha with Franco earlier. Natasha is a similar height and build to Caroline. She may have been helping Franco and Hale with this appeal. You said it had been recorded earlier?'

McGuire nodded. 'Or she could simply be involved with Franco Lanzi *and* his wife's murder.'

Pearl slowly shook her head.

'You're ruling him out now?' asked McGuire. 'After seeing them together like that – twice?'

Troubled, Pearl reminded him, 'I told you. Franco had a perfectly reasonable excuse for his meeting with Natasha the other morning. He said he had explained to her that Caroline had gone missing and he needed to know if Natasha had seen her . . . You're right that two of the most common motives for murder are love and money but . . . I still need to keep an open mind. Look!' she exclaimed, as the image on the TV screen shifted from the body double treading the allotment path to the TV studio. Hale was staring directly into the camera as he continued with the appeal.

'We are also keen to identify and talk to a person who may have been at the allotments on Sunday evening, just before eight p.m. It's important that we're able to eliminate this person from our enquiries.' Looking increasingly shiny under the studio lighting, he loosened his tie, then swallowed hard.

'He's nervous,' Pearl observed.

'He's been watching too many cop shows.'

'Well, you can't say he's not trying.'

'Trying to make a name for himself.'

'To keep hold of *your* job.'

McGuire knew Pearl was right. He had another gulp of Oyster Stout, trying hard not to think of how his own superintendent, Maurice Welch, resented every minute that McGuire, the DFL, had remained in his force beyond the original deadline of his secondment. But once Pearl had crossed his path, McGuire knew he could never return to London – or his former life. At the time, he had been investigating what had appeared to be an accidental death, although Pearl had sensed otherwise – and had been proved correct. McGuire had underestimated her but why would he have expected that a cook and restaurateur could match or even eclipse his own abilities for crime-solving?

'Clues for a murder are like ingredients for a recipe,' she had told him. 'Put them together in the right way and the results can be very satisfying.' She had said that in the local Hotel Continental, in the same bar in which McGuire had sampled his first Oyster Stout and had quickly developed a taste for the beer – and Pearl. McGuire now eyed the bottle in his hand and realised something. 'Welch must have agreed to this appeal,' he said. 'Even though it's unlikely to produce any meaningful results.'

Pearl turned to him. 'Why do you say that?'

McGuire indicated the TV. 'Hale's after eye-witness reports, but you know yourself the allotment's off the beaten track, and away from the main route of Joy Lane. Jackie reported to me that there's no clear view of the allotments from the rear of any of the neighbouring houses . . . You said you felt someone was watching you when you arrived?'

Pearl nodded.

McGuire went on: 'And that person made off as soon as you got near the composter?'

'I think so.'

'Then it's my guess that they *had* to be the killer. Why else haven't they come forward?'

'Maybe they will,' she said, allowing her words to hang between them until her attention was captured once more by the TV camera homing in on Franco Lanzi.

'He looks much smarter than I've seen him lately,' she said. He was wearing a stylish grey jacket with an open-neck shirt. His silver hair was tamed and he looked less tired, though Pearl realised that might well have had something to do with the TV make-up department. He stared straight into the camera as he spoke slowly and carefully.

'My wife was my world,' he began, 'my love . . . but she's been taken from me by this killer, who must be found.' He was silent for what seemed far too long. Then he continued: 'If you have any information at all, I urge you—' He rephrased his words: 'I *beg* you,' he continued, 'please contact the police on the number they will give you.' Looking back at Hale and DS Bates beside him, he allowed the detective to take up the thread.

'And that number is . . .' Hale indicated the digits flashing up on the screen. He assured viewers that all calls would be treated in strictest confidence. A moment later, the newsreader reappeared with further local news: a runaway pig, from a local farm, had been captured.

Pearl switched down the volume, repeating softly, almost to herself, 'My world . . . my love.'

McGuire commented. 'Doesn't sound much like the woman you described?'

Pearl agreed. 'No, but then I'm not Franco Lanzi.'

McGuire sighed and flapped a hand towards the television screen. 'You know, the only consolation in all this . . . is that you weren't actually named in that report as the person who found the body.'

Aware that this was true, she turned to him and McGuire recognised the look in her eyes. It signalled a need for comfort so he slipped his arm around her, allowing her to move closer to him. As her head sank onto his shoulder, she felt safe and secure in his embrace – in spite of the brutal murder.

CHAPTER NINETEEN

'You two seem to be getting on,' said Dolly, in the restaurant the next day as she assembled some potted shrimps on wafer-thin slices of brown bread. It was one of the few culinary tasks Pearl entrusted to her mother, whose many talents failed to include cookery. Instead, Pearl preferred to make best use of her front of house, as Dolly knew most of the restaurant's local customers.

'Is that surprising?' asked Pearl.

'You're usually at loggerheads during a case,' Dolly reminded her.

'Well,' Pearl began, 'that's because the case is usually McGuire's, and he thinks I'm interfering, but this new DI, Hale, has taken over, remember?'

She moved to the cooker and began stirring the lunchtime special she had been preparing all morning, her own take on a Marseille bouillabaisse featuring John Dory, turbot, mullet and gilthead bream. It was usual for Pearl to transform an established recipe, using it only as a foundation to build on, much as a jazz musician uses a simple tune as the basis for improvisation. Bending over the pan, she took in the smell of garlic, bay, fennel and *bouquet garni*, then turned down the heat to a gentle simmer.

Dolly observed her daughter, proud of Pearl's culinary expertise, and her natural beauty, on display this morning as she stood near the window in the morning light, a shaft of summer sun falling on her like a spotlight. Pearl took after her father with her tall, willowy frame while Dolly was short and stout, and constantly battled with her weight. Considering herself a blank canvas for self-expression, Dolly had assumed a mantle of flamboyance, dyeing her hair a myriad of different colours and seizing the chance to wear resplendent items from a lifetime's collection of ostentatious clothes and junk jewellery. In contrast, Pearl shied away from necklaces and bracelets, refusing to wear rings, which might be lost in restaurant dishes during their preparation. In fact, these days, she seemed only to treasure a simple pair of natural pearl earrings that McGuire had given to her and which she wore only on special occasions.

With her long dark hair routinely pinned up for work at The Whitstable Pearl, the restaurant environment always offered Pearl an excuse to adopt her simple style, although Dolly had long recognised that her daughter's love of vintage dresses, bought for comfort and practicality, represented a rejection of her mother's extravagance. The truth lay somewhere in between, but Pearl always managed to look striking whatever she wore.

'You mean,' said Dolly, 'the Flat Foot on TV last night?' She sighed, remembering something. 'I must say I felt for Franco when he made that plea for information.'

'So did I,' said Pearl. 'You know, I can't help thinking that if he did have something to do with his wife's murder he must be a very good actor.'

'Well,' said Dolly, 'he certainly had ambitions at one time.'

'Oh?' said Pearl, giving her mother her full attention.

Finishing the last of her potted-shrimp starters, Dolly wiped her hands on her apron. 'He did catwalk modelling, for one of the Italian fashion houses. Appeared in a few of their aftershave ads for magazines and TV. But then he got a part in an Italian film. An arthouse movie.' She thought for a moment, then gave up. 'Don't ask me what the title was but he must have fancied acting as a new career and failed to make the grade.'

'And this was before he met Caroline?'

'Oh yes.'

Pearl became thoughtful. 'Victor Bessant said he'd been an artist at one time . . . so perhaps that's *two* men who failed to make the grade?'

'I don't know much about Bessant,' said Dolly, 'except that he seems to know the art market.'

'He has some of Joe's work now too.'

'Yes, I noticed that,' said Dolly, thoughtful. 'I saw the carvings in the gallery window this morning, but

I wouldn't have thought they were Bessant's favoured style.' She confided: 'Trevor, who did the lovely seascape that was donated to the carnival fundraiser, said Bessant's usual interest is in fine-art pieces – large canvases, not sculpture or wood.'

'Well,' said Pearl, 'Florence said it had been Natasha who'd recommended Joe's work to him, remember?'

'That's right,' Dolly recalled. 'But from what I've seen so far, I can't imagine Victor Bessant gives much weight to his wife's opinion. If you ask me, the poor woman seems a bit of a hectored trophy wife, dragged around to private views and other social events.'

Pearl considered this before replacing the lid on her pan of bouillabaisse. Perhaps there were similarities in Franco's role with Caroline, and this was something else he and Natasha Bessant might have in common. Choosing to change the subject, she said: 'You mentioned that Michael had talked to you about Vanessa.'

Dolly nodded. 'That was after Caroline's meeting on Saturday,' she said. 'He really didn't like the possibility of Vanessa having to get rid of those hens. And now, of course, she's lost one. Poor thing.'

'The hen or Vanessa?'

'Both,' said Dolly, moving to the sink to wash her hands.

'Yes,' said Pearl. 'Michael seems incredibly protective of her. They've grown very close. And seem perfectly suited.' She thought for a moment. 'And in spite of

Caroline's death,' she continued, 'all those complaints are still live.'

Dolly looked back from the sink. 'Still lodged with the council, you mean?'

'Unresolved as yet. And did I tell you I also found out from Peter Radcliffe yesterday that they were all sent anonymously?'

'Cowardly,' Dolly muttered, as she dried her hands.

'Which seems very unlike Caroline,' said Pearl. 'She was anything *but* a coward and she *did* deny knowing anything about them, remember?'

Dolly approached. 'You're . . . seriously thinking they were sent by someone else?' At Pearl's silence, Dolly frowned. 'Who? The Bessants?' she suggested. 'They didn't receive any complaint.'

Pearl was unconvinced. 'I don't think Victor Bessant would shy away from making a direct complaint either.'

'Marty didn't receive one?'

Pearl shook her head. 'It's also not Marty's style to lodge an anonymous complaint. In any case, he's far too busy trying to become a vegetable millionaire, and if he was upset about any of the things that were complained about, I'm sure we'd have heard long before.'

'Yes,' Dolly agreed, pensive. 'But the allotments aren't overlooked,' she began, 'so who on earth would be bothered by what goes on there other than other plot holders?'

Pearl gave this some thought. 'Perhaps the person *wasn't* bothered.'

'You mean they just had it in for us?'

'Or *one* of us,' said Pearl.

'I'm not quite sure what you're saying.'

Pearl was just about to explain when her phone rang. She indicated that it was McGuire calling, then wiped her hands on her apron and took the call. 'How are you today?' she asked.

'In a state of shock.'

Pearl's smile faded. 'Why – what's happened?'

Dolly leaned closer to hear what McGuire had to say.

'Hale has made an arrest.'

Pearl gasped. 'You mean . . . following the appeal last night?'

'That's right,' McGuire confirmed. 'It seems two dog walkers came forward with eye-witness information corroborating that just before eight p.m. on Sunday evening, someone was seen hurrying away from the allotments and up onto the railway embankment.'

'So I *wasn't* mistaken that someone else was there when I arrived.'

'Seems not,' said McGuire. 'And that same person was not only seen but identified.'

'Who?' asked Pearl, as Dolly craned her neck to hear more.

McGuire paused for a second before replying: 'Ted Rowden.'

CHAPTER TWENTY

'I don't understand,' said Vanessa Hobbs, looking strained as she sat with Michael Stopes at a lunchtime table in The Whitstable Pearl. 'Are you saying that the police believe Ted murdered Caroline?'

Pearl lowered her voice so that customers enjoying bouillabaisse on nearby tables wouldn't hear. 'All I know is, he's been arrested.'

'Arrested?' echoed Michael. 'That's serious.'

'Not necessarily,' Pearl explained. 'The police may have done that for Ted's benefit as much as their own. He'll be questioned under caution, in effect warned that what he tells them—'

'Could be used against him.' Michael nodded impatiently. 'Understood. But he was definitely seen leaving the allotment?'

'Apparently so,' said Pearl. 'Ted's a familiar figure around town. Lots of people know him.'

'That's right,' said Vanessa. 'He's a lovely old gentleman.'

Michael seemed perplexed. 'But if he didn't have anything to do with the murder why on earth did he lie about being there?'

Before Pearl could answer she noticed Ruby juggling bowls of bouillabaisse alone. 'Look, I have to get back to work now,' she said, 'but I've called a meeting. This evening. Six thirty at Seaspray Cottage. The others can make it. Can you?'

'We certainly can,' said Michael.

'Good,' said Pearl, with a satisfied smile.

Straight after the restaurant had finished its lunchtime service, Pearl dropped in at Cornucopia on her way back to Seaspray Cottage and found Marty holding court with some Berlin tourists. He was showing off a new juicing machine that his staff were using to make fresh smoothies. The Berliners sipped from their glasses, as Marty expounded on the health benefits of his fruit, then lined up to pose for photos by the machine.

Eventually Marty sidled up to Pearl. 'So,' he began, in a low voice, 'I hear the police have got their man?'

'No,' said Pearl, forcefully. 'For the time being they happen to have Ted for questioning.'

Marty moved closer. 'And we all know why,' he whispered furtively. 'Escaping from the scene of the crime?'

Pearl rolled her eyes. 'I've no doubt that Ted will be released once the police recognise he's no killer.' From her bag she produced an order for restaurant produce, which Marty plucked from her hand. 'Well, I know you're fond of Ted,' he began, 'but you really shouldn't let personal feelings cloud your judgement, Pearl.' Loading a cart with her order, he went on: 'Ted was very put out by that complaint about his bees. He's had them a very long time.'

'I know,' said Pearl.

'And he's aware he was breaking the rules,' said Marty.

Pearl looked sharply at him. 'It's not against the rules to keep bees on that allotment.'

'That's right,' Marty agreed. 'But it *is* against the rules to sell any produce grown there.'

'Are you saying Ted's been selling his honey?'

Marty gave a slow nod. 'As a matter of fact,' he went on, 'he came to me to ask if I'd stock some.'

'Ted wanted you to sell his Rowden's Honey?'

Marty moved to his counter and slid a hand beneath it, retrieving a jar, which he handed to Pearl. 'Different name,' he announced, indicating the label, which featured no information other than the brand name, Whitstable Honey, above an image of a hive.

'No manufacturer's name or address,' Pearl noted. 'And you've been selling this for Ted?'

'I couldn't, could I? *I'd* be breaking the rules. But I felt for the old fella so I bought a few jars for myself.' He moved closer. 'It's no secret that you use a few things you've grown on your plot in your restaurant dishes.' He gave her a playful nudge. 'No one could do you for that, but council regulations clearly state that we can't sell produce grown on our allotments.' He added: 'They don't say anything about *buying* it. Get my drift? So that's what I did.' He continued: 'Ted's had that allotment for nearly fifty years, passed down to him by his uncle Wally. You know how much it means to him. He's there almost every day, but if he thought someone had planned to dob him in with the council, well . . .' He raised his groomed eyebrows.

Pearl computed what Marty had just revealed, then shook her head. 'Ted isn't a killer.'

'So you say, Pearl. But can you *really* be sure of that?' Marty asked. 'And do any of us really know what we're capable of when we're pushed to the limit?'

Pearl's gaze lowered to the jar of honey in her hand. 'How many more of these have you got?'

'Just that one,' Marty said. 'I finished the rest – and very nice it was too.'

'Can I have this?'

'Sure.' Marty gave a sad smile. 'Shame if it ends up being the old fella's last jar.'

Some time later, Pearl was seated in front of her laptop in Seaspray Cottage, pausing for a moment to take a look beyond her window at the beach. In the distance, to the east, bleached wind-farm sails turned slowly on the breeze, new neighbours for the rusting towers of the Red Sands army fort that had sat eight miles offshore since the Second World War. Closer in, a kite surfer was performing impressive somersaults in front of a crowd on the beach – mainly families and pet dogs enjoying the fine weather.

Pearl allowed herself to imagine sailing out to take full advantage of the steady southerly breeze, perhaps even persuading McGuire to come with her to orbit the old fort or catch sight of a seal colony that seemed to be enjoying the local estuary waters and the sheltered channel known as the Swale. She had been prevented from enjoying all of these things with him this summer due to the accident that had forced him into the wretched blue cast. Pearl had come to despise it as much as McGuire did, because as well as depriving her of precious time with him, it had also robbed the detective of the satisfaction of his work.

Pearl understood McGuire's frustration, the intrinsic need to restore justice and create order from chaos by solving an insoluble mystery. But now there was another mystery to solve – a murder committed within Pearl's community, and on McGuire's patch – a mystery with which Pearl had made little progress while McGuire found himself excluded from the formal investigation. What information he had gleaned so far had come from the morsels of intelligence he had managed to extract from DS Jackie Bates, the attractive sergeant who had taken Pearl's initial statement and who seemed more than willing to feed titbits of information about Hale's case to McGuire. Pearl guessed that McGuire might be with Bates at this very moment, attempting to gain a further update on Hale's investigation in general, and Ted Rowden's place in it in particular.

She closed her eyes, hoping that Ted had agreed to a duty solicitor during his questioning: that would ensure he understood the importance of his right to remain silent. Marty's words now echoed in her mind, taking over the playful soundtrack on the beach beyond her window: *'Ted's had that allotment for nearly fifty years, passed down to him by his uncle Wally . . . You know how much it means to him. He's there almost every day . . . If he thought someone had planned to dob him in with the council, well, do any of us really know what we're capable of when pushed to the limit?'*

Pearl opened her eyes and focused again on her laptop screen. She had managed to undertake a fair bit of research in the last hour: first on Victor Bessant, who, she discovered, had gained a degree in fine art at Camberwell School of Art in the early nineties, before taking off to live in France and Spain where he had mounted a few exhibitions of his work. A long hiatus had followed – and his marriage to Natasha – before he had resurfaced on the London art scene, this time as a gallery owner. Images stored on stock-photo library sites showed exhibition previews with shots that included Caroline and Franco Lanzi. Pearl supposed they may have been taken while Caroline had represented Victor as one of her PR clients. Slipping on her glasses, Pearl studied them carefully, searching for any evidence of over-familiarity between Franco and Natasha – the tell-tale signs McGuire had admonished her for being unsure about: *'You surely know the signs by now, Pearl.'*

'Signs?'

'The kind of look that passes between two people when they're . . .'

Holding Pearl's gaze, McGuire had leaned closer and Pearl closed her eyes again, remembering his kiss, savouring it in her mind before she opened her eyes once more and carefully re-examined the photos before her. They showed nothing more than Franco and Natasha Bessant, champagne flutes in hand, smiling, almost professionally, for the camera while Victor and Caroline seemed engaged in conversation. As Pearl scrolled through the images she couldn't help but note that Natasha and Franco were astonishingly photogenic, which spurred her on to search for footage from the film Franco had been in. It took a while to find on a social-media site, but finally Pearl clicked on a link to an old Italian movie called *Inferno e Notte*.

A quick language search translated this as *Hell and Night*, a suitable title for a film in which Franco had taken the role of a young Florentine involved in a torturous and steamy relationship with an attractive young woman of equally dubious acting talent. Pearl marvelled at her mother's ability to retain such trivia, but Dolly had always been a fan of European cinema having once been a member of a local film-appreciation group. Unfortunately, Dolly's contributions to any further background information on Pearl's new client had ended as abruptly as Franco Lanzi's film career. Nonetheless, this discovery went some way to establishing that, at one time, Franco must have believed he possessed talent as an actor – and it remained possible that his talent might have been useful during a murder investigation . . .

As if on cue, Pearl's phone rang. Without checking the caller ID, she answered it, and was surprised to hear her son's voice on the line.

'Mum?'

'Charlie,' Pearl began, concerned by his tone. 'Is everything all right?'

'Everything here, yes,' said Charlie. 'But not with you. I just heard about the murder.'

Pearl had wanted to keep this news from him. 'Who told you?'

'A friend in Whitstable,' said Charlie. 'She happened to see an appeal on the local news last night. So what's going on? Is Mike on the case?'

'No,' said Pearl. 'He had an accident—'

'What kind of—'

'Nothing serious,' said Pearl, 'but he's in plaster at the moment.'

'Doesn't sound great,' said Charlie. 'Is it safe at the allotment or is there some crazy killer on the loose?'

'The police are investigating.'

Charlie saw through his mother's all too concise reply. 'Tell me you're not involved?'

Pearl took a deep breath. 'Look, Charlie—'

'You are.' He spoke over her. 'I should've known, shouldn't I? If a murder happens in Whitstable you won't be far away.'

'I'm not in any danger.'

'That you know of. But once you start digging and getting closer to whoever did this, you will be. It stands to reason . . . Is Mike there with you?'

'No.'

'Then I'm coming home. Now.'

'Charlie, there's really no need,' said Pearl, pushing a hand through her hair. 'I promise you I'm not taking any risks. I'm just helping the local police with their enquiries. That's all.' She took her time, then asked, 'How is it there? Are you still having fun?'

'I was until today,' said Charlie glumly.

'Then carry on,' said Pearl, 'and don't worry.' Glancing at the time on her laptop screen, she added: 'Look I have to meet friends soon. They're coming here.'

'So you won't be alone?' said Charlie.

'No,' Pearl said softly. 'I'm fine.'

A pause followed. Then, 'Mum?'

'Yes?'

'I love you.'

Pearl softened. 'I love you too, Charlie.'

After the call ended, Pearl sat, listening to the sounds of children playing on the beach beyond her window. Her eyes drifted to a photo she always kept on a table in her sitting room showing Charlie with herself, when he was little more than a toddler, on the beach, waving a flag he had just won after a crabbing competition during a local oyster festival.

It seemed impossible to accept that Charlie was now a young man, suitably concerned about his mother. Pearl had always recognised Carl in her son, their pursuit of art, and lately he was also displaying far more of his father's physical characteristics: fair hair, a winning smile, an athletic build, as though his parents' genes were now vying for supremacy. Pearl had always expected that one day Charlie might require more details about his absent parent but until now what he knew seemed to suffice – either that, or he wasn't owning up to more curiosity.

Pearl's phone rang again. Expecting it to be Charlie once more, she answered quickly – to hear Franco Lanzi's voice on the line.

'Is it true the police have arrested the old man?'

'Yes,' said Pearl. 'But only for questioning.'

'Why didn't you tell me?'

'Because I'm waiting for more information.'

'They say he was seen leaving the allotment just before you found Caro's body.'

'They?' echoed Pearl.

'Victor and Natasha.'

Pearl was brought up short. 'They probably heard that from their neighbour, Councillor Radcliffe,' she said, almost to herself. 'Look,' she continued, 'small towns like ours are known for being hotbeds of rumour and half-truths . . . At a time like this you can also add a fairy tale or two to the list.'

'Are you telling me he's *not* a suspect?' asked Franco.

Pearl collected her thoughts. 'I imagine that those of us who have grievances about the complaints are *all* considered suspects . . . together with those who knew her well.'

'Like me?' said Franco. 'You're not suggesting *I* could have murdered my wife? I *hired* you to find her—'

'Which I did,' Pearl reminded him.

'And the person who killed her?'

'I promise you,' said Pearl, 'I won't rest until I find who is responsible.' A pause followed on the line before Pearl spoke again. 'In fact, I've called a meeting of the allotment holders tonight. At six thirty.'

'Where?'

'Here at my home. I thought it would be best that we meet out of the public eye – especially now the press are involved. If you feel able to come along—'

Franco's voice cut in: 'I'll be there.'

The line went dead in Pearl's hand.

CHAPTER TWENTY-ONE

By six thirty Pearl's invited guests had arrived at Seaspray Cottage, apart from her mother and Madge. Dolly had once again agreed to give her friend a lift, and the pair arrived fashionably late, within a quarter of an hour of the others.

Pearl had been honest in explaining to Franco Lanzi why she was staging the meeting at her home: the recent police TV appeal had thrust Caroline's murder into the glare of publicity, so it would be wise to avoid undue attention, for Franco in particular, at local establishments like the Old Neptune and The Whitstable Pearl. Privately, Pearl also felt that at Seaspray Cottage, without Cindy and Russ having been invited, she would also avoid any further fracas between David and his wife's lover. Not only that, it would be easier for her to monitor David Chappell's drinking, especially in the light of all that his wife had confided to Pearl on the beach. In truth, she felt that the young woman's comments had been less 'confidences' than a bold admission of her husband's alcoholism, which had led to instances of domestic rage, if not violence. It also seemed clear to Pearl that if David harboured hope of Cindy returning to him, it was seriously misplaced. Cindy had spoken of wanting a divorce, as well as a fair financial share of a marital home, which she intended to use to create a new future with Russ Parker. The couple seemed unashamedly in love, with Russ having proudly assumed the role of Cindy's protector, a role Michael Stopes also seemed to have taken on for Vanessa.

As with the meeting that had taken place at the Lanzis' home on the night before Caroline's murder, Michael and Vanessa had arrived together and now sat close to one another on a bench in Pearl's sea-facing garden. No doubt, thought Pearl, the pair had found initial common ground through their shared commitment to their professions. Michael was known to be a responsible and gifted teacher, and Vanessa was much loved by the children she cared for at the local nursery. If further evidence was needed of Vanessa's caring nature it was surely in the form of the hens she had rescued from the battery farm – and whose fate had been threatened by the complaint to the council.

It was yet another warm evening, with only a light breeze blowing offshore, so Pearl had made use of the seating surrounding her beach-hut office, and her patio table, around which sat Natasha and Victor Bessant with Franco Lanzi – all looking pensive, unlike Florence and

Joe who arrived in an unusually bright mood, with news of sales interest in Joe's work. 'It really is wonderful,' Florence whispered, shrugging off a light jacket and handing it to Pearl, 'but in the midst of this awful tragedy, two of Joe's carvings have sold already – the snails and the python.' She gabbled on excitedly, reminding Pearl of a burbling stream. 'I can't tell you what this means – we've been struggling for so long, especially after losing the workshop and facing problems with the council over our studio. It's as though we've finally been given a reprieve.'

Joe sauntered off towards the garden, leaving Florence with Pearl. 'I honestly believe he was close to giving up, you know. He even talked about looking for a job because—'

'Flo?' Joe called from the patio door, causing her to break off. She glanced across at him, relieved when he gave her a benign smile, which she returned, before turning back to Pearl. 'Sorry,' she said, embarrassed now. 'Joe always thinks I go on too much. And he's right.'

With that, she hurried across to join him, moving out into the garden where Dolly and Madge had just arrived, via the promenade, to sit together in two rattan armchairs.

Marty had taken a bench seat and was enjoying some of Pearl's tapas. The only guest who seemed unable to settle was David Chappell, who stood at a distance from everyone else, staring out to sea, as though he wished he was somewhere else.

Once Pearl was sure she had everyone's attention she welcomed her guests and began to explain why she had invited them. 'I thought it would be helpful, useful to us, *and* to the police investigation, if we got together this evening and—'

'Compared notes?' said Marty, helping himself to some of Pearl's smoked salmon *crostini*.

'Shared information,' said Pearl.

'Good idea!' said Madge. 'And I, for one, would like to know what's happening with Ted and how we can bust him out of jail.'

'He's only been arrested – not imprisoned,' said Marty.

'*Wrongfully* arrested,' said Madge. 'He's no more a murderer than I am,' she insisted. 'The rozzers have got the wrong man. Free the Whitstable One, I say!'

'Madge has a point,' agreed Dolly. 'Ted's been in custody now for how long?'

'Still less than twenty-four hours,' said Pearl. 'And the police can only hold him for that length of time without more evidence to charge him. As far as I'm aware, no charges have been brought. He's simply helping them with their enquiries.'

'After being identified at the scene of the crime?' said Michael, sceptically.

'*Near* the scene of the crime,' Pearl clarified. 'I understand two dog walkers say they saw him heading up to the embankment on Sunday evening.'

'From the allotment?' asked Natasha.

'Apparently so,' said Pearl.

Victor Bessant scowled. 'And he failed to mention this before?'

'So he lied!' said Franco. 'Why would he do that if he didn't have something to hide?'

'That's right,' said David Chappell, suddenly. All eyes turned to him as he came forward to join the others. 'Why would anyone want to lie to the police about this? After all,' he said, 'a woman is dead.' He looked at Pearl who in turn glanced away, knowing he was reminding her that she had hardly been open with Hale, and had been seen by Chappell at the rear of the Lanzis' house after the fateful meeting on Saturday evening.

'David's right,' she said. 'Someone murdered Caroline – a member of our community and a neighbour.'

'My customer!' said Marty, aggrieved.

'Yes,' Pearl went on, 'and I think it's time we were *all* open with the police *and* with each other. I know the investigating officer will be considering whether any of us may have held a grievance against Caroline.'

Vanessa piped up: 'About the complaints, you mean? No one could possibly think that one of us committed murder because of that.'

Victor Bessant gave some thought to this before he decided: 'It's probably just a case of eliminating suspects from their enquiries.'

'Narrowing the field of the investigation, you mean?' said Joe.

Victor gave a tight nod but Franco said: 'And exactly *who* has been eliminated?'

'I don't know,' said Pearl. 'As far as I'm aware none of us has a firm alibi for the night of the murder.'

Florence seemed confused. 'But I told you, and the police, Joe was with me.'

'And I was with Vanessa,' said Michael.

'I could say the same about Natasha and myself,' put in Victor, 'but that's pretty meaningless as far as the police are concerned. Why wouldn't a husband or wife protect their spouse?'

Pearl noted David's reaction to this. Looking bereft, his gaze fell on a bottle of wine sitting on the table and his hands clenched as if they had been ordered to remain at his sides.

'But we're not all married,' said Madge. 'And we're not all lunatics either.'

'Someone murdered my wife!' said Franco.

'And the police will discover who did this,' said Pearl.

'And if they don't,' he said, turning to her, 'you will.'

Pearl paused. 'I've told you, I'll do my best.'

'And you should also do your best to get Ted out of Canterbury police station!' said Madge.

'The police have due processes,' said Pearl.

'They also have the wrong man,' Madge insisted.

'Or do they?' asked David, as if remembering something. 'On the night of the meeting Ted used a mobility scooter for transport.'

'So?' said Joe.

'So,' David continued, 'when he was seen making his way up the embankment to escape Pearl he was on foot.'

Dolly shook her head. 'Those dog walkers must have been mistaken. Ted has arthritis.'

Vanessa suddenly spoke: 'But he's no invalid, Dolly. In fact, he's very fit for his age.'

'He certainly works hard at the allotment,' said Michael.

'But he can't walk long distances,' said Madge, firmly.

'And yet,' Joe began, 'if he was seen, he must have walked to the allotment that night – and then walked all the way home. He lives in Windsor House – so that's over half a mile each way.'

He looked at Florence, who commented, '*And* he didn't take the mobility scooter.'

'He doesn't need it *all* the time,' said Madge. 'He just uses it like a car – for convenience. His arthritis comes and goes. It's always worse in damp weather. How could you possibly think he could've done this?'

Vanessa tried to dismiss the idea. 'Madge is right. Ted's not a killer. He may have had a complaint made against him but so did the rest of us.'

'Not *all* of us,' said Marty.

'That's true,' Victor agreed.

Vanessa looked troubled. 'Caroline insisted she knew nothing about the complaints.'

Franco spoke up in frustration: 'And she was telling the truth! My wife didn't make any complaints. She would have told me.'

'Then who did make the complaints?' asked David. He waited for a response. Finally Pearl gave it. 'They were all sent anonymously.'

Madge's jaw dropped. 'Like poison-pen letters, you mean?'

'In a way,' said Pearl. 'They certainly had the effect of making us think that Caroline must have been to blame.'

Vanessa's hand moved to her throat. 'You mean . . . so that someone was *provoked* to murder her?'

'If so, it was for *no* reason,' said Franco, bitterly, staring around the garden as though searching for an explanation. A hush fell. In the next instant, David Chappell stepped forward and poured himself a glass of wine. Pearl watched as he clutched the glass, appeared to struggle with himself and set it down on the table.

As he did so, Pearl's doorbell rang. Excusing herself, she moved quickly inside, heading across the living room to open her front door where she found two figures standing in the shadows. McGuire, propped on his crutches, was easily identifiable, but the second figure moved into the light before Pearl recognised who it was.

'Ted . . .' she said, as the old man raised a smile.

McGuire moved forward. 'They had to let him go.'

CHAPTER TWENTY-TWO

The next day brought more fine weather, cotton balls of white cloud scudding across an azure sky as Pearl sat with McGuire enjoying breakfast with him on her patio.

'I bet Ted's relieved to be waking up in his own bed this morning,' she said, stirring a teaspoonful of the old beekeeper's Whitstable Honey into her tea.

McGuire looked across at her and said softly: 'I was pleased not to wake up in mine.' He winked.

Pearl leaned closer to pour him some coffee. 'It was good of DS Bates to tip you off that Ted was going to be released.'

McGuire offered no reply as he bit into one of Pearl's marmalade-filled croissants.

'Jackie Bates has been very helpful to you but what exactly is in it for her?' she asked. Her head was tipped inquisitively to one side.

'There's camaraderie among fellow officers,' he replied.

'Especially the attractive ones?'

He couldn't help smiling. 'Are those beautiful grey eyes of yours turning green again?'

'Well,' said Pearl, 'you don't think she could be leading you into some kind of trap?'

'With Hale?' McGuire shook his head, dismissing the idea. 'I'm glad she's working with him,' he confessed. 'She's a good DS.'

He sipped his coffee while Pearl imagined how she would have felt if McGuire had ever been able to say the same about her.

McGuire reached across to pour himself some more coffee, hoping it would help him negotiate Pearl's mood this morning. He knew she was disappointed with their progress in this case but he also sensed her insecurity about his relationship with Bates. In spite of their usual sparring, which he had come to expect with the cases they had shared, there always seemed to be new obstacles in the way, of one sort or another. At one point it had been Dolly. She had initially been spiky with him, nicknaming him Flat Foot and doing her best to prevent Pearl becoming involved with a police officer – 'lackeys of the state', as she was apt to describe them – before she had finally succumbed to McGuire's charm. Considering Pearl's own independent spirit, and need to go her own way, McGuire had never thought Dolly to be too much of a problem – but there had also been Charlie to think about. Fortunately Pearl's son had seemed willing to accept McGuire from the start, and living in Canterbury meant that the two were neighbours and could even meet for an occasional beer.

The real problem, McGuire realised, had been Pearl herself because on an emotional level there always seemed to be something in the way. McGuire knew that Pearl sometimes pulled up a drawbridge to protect herself, but he was also aware that he was guilty of this too. But having come this far, he now had no wish to put a foot wrong. He decided to tread carefully and try to distract her with the case in hand.

'Jackie just tipped me off that Hale had nothing on Ted, so he was being released. I told you, the old fella was pretty clued up. He opted for a solicitor, took his right to silence seriously and clammed up. Hale didn't have enough to keep him any longer.'

'Aside from the eyewitness reports,' said Pearl. 'They proved that Ted lied about not being at the allotment at the time of Caroline's death.'

McGuire shook his head. 'Still not enough to hold him,' he insisted. 'The guy's eighty years old, Pearl. He got confused. Claims he only went back for something he'd left behind.'

Pearl frowned. 'But I told you David Chappell asked why Ted hadn't used his mobility scooter.'

'Well, he wouldn't have, would he?' said McGuire. 'It was his glasses he'd forgotten – and he can't drive without them. In any case,' McGuire added, after taking a sip of his coffee, 'why's Chappell suddenly asking questions like that? Trying to deflect attention from himself again?'

'I don't know. Perhaps I'm not sure of anything – especially about David being an out-of-control alcoholic.'

McGuire set down his coffee cup. 'Then why would Cindy give you that impression if it wasn't true?'

Pearl gave this some thought. 'Perhaps it justifies her decision to leave him – or perhaps she enjoys having the protection of Russ.' She realised: 'Cindy and Russ are two people we've failed to factor into all this.'

'Is it significant they returned just before all this happened?'

'Maybe, but I just can't see how they can be connected to the murder,' said Pearl. 'They have a perfect alibi – they were in the bar of the Marine Hotel after arriving from Margate. I checked with the staff – they can't possibly have been involved.' She set down her cup. 'But I keep returning to the fact that David Chappell went into that blind rage about the prospect of losing his allotment plot. And it's true he's been drinking heavily – I saw all the empties in his recycling box. He did say that getting back to his plot was his way of moving forward and suddenly he was faced with losing it.' She turned to McGuire. 'He seemed very sure that Caroline was behind that – but we all were.'

She reached into her bag and took out one of the leaflets given to her by Cindy, advertising Russ Parker's professional skills. 'Do you think you can possibly look into Russ's finances?'

McGuire shrugged. 'I'll try, but from everything you've just said, it still looks to me as though David Chappell was the one with most to lose.'

As McGuire continued his breakfast, Pearl stared out to sea, finding it hard to disagree.

A few hours later, after finishing the lunchtime service at the restaurant, Pearl headed along Harbour Street on her way back to Seaspray Cottage, keen to exchange the stifling heat of the restaurant for a stroll along the airy coastline. The town was packed with those who rejected the chance of sampling the pleasures of Whitstable's pebbled beach; groups of sightseers and shoppers who, with plenty of time on their hands, always moved at an entirely different pace from local people. When they weren't congregating around the windows of the town's eclectic mix of quirky independent shops, which offered all manner of items from connoisseur cheese to vintage vinyl, the tourists seemed to shuffle about, while townspeople moved at an altogether brisker tempo, weaving an efficient route around the tourists on the pavement. Pearl was doing just that, when she happened to pass the Bessants' gallery and caught sight of its window in which none of Joe Fuller's pieces now remained. Instead, the space had been taken up by another fine painting, this time depicting the Old Neptune pub at night.

At that very moment, Natasha exited, brought up short to see Pearl before her. Instantly, she offered a warm smile, which Pearl returned as she remarked: 'I couldn't help noticing the new window.' Natasha glanced at the painting on display.

'That's right. The last of Joe's pieces sold today. Victor's very pleased.'

'Not as pleased as Joe and Florence, I'll bet,' said Pearl. 'They really needed those sales.'

Natasha shrugged. 'Well, for what it's worth, I never had any doubt that Joe's work would fly. As soon as I saw some of his carvings at the allotment, I tried to tell Victor what a talented sculptor he is.'

'Tried?' said Pearl, picking up on the word.

Natasha shrugged. 'I don't always manage to convince him. Victor likes to reach his own decisions in his own time.'

'I'm sure,' said Pearl, glancing through the window into the gallery to see Victor talking animatedly to a prospective customer. Looking back at Natasha, she asked: 'Do you have time for a coffee?'

Natasha smiled. 'Of course.'

Five minutes later, Pearl and Natasha had arrived at the nearby harbour where fishing boats seemed to be jostling for space, halyards clanking as though providing percussion for a band playing on the stage of what was known as South Quay.

Pearl paid a coffee vendor and handed Natasha a beaker of cappuccino, then indicated that they might move closer to the music and sit on a bench that faced out to sea.

'Always such a lively place, isn't it?' said Natasha.

'In the summer,' Pearl agreed, stirring her tea. She glanced around the harbour, taking in the crowds ambling around a marketplace consisting of local traders selling their wares from mock beach huts.

'You're used to all this,' said Natasha, 'but for me it's still very new and colourful.'

'Yes, I'm sure,' Pearl replied. 'It's true we locals don't always fully appreciate what's on our own doorstep. Visitors come and explore the whole area but I haven't wandered very far for a while, and I can't remember the last time I swam in the sea.' She sipped her tea.

'Too busy with your restaurant?' said Natasha.

'And other things.' Pearl glanced away, her attention drawn to an area of the harbour known as Dead Man's Corner, so named because all that fell into the sea locally was said to wash up there. Some years ago, the city council had reached an agreement with a local trust to improve that stretch of harbour. An architect had been commissioned to design a large deck with wooden seating on which members of the public could relax and 'watch harbour life go by'. It had been hoped that the development might help to change the area's nickname for something less macabre, but the construction of a gabion wall only served to make it more fitting as it was filled with various dried flotsam and jetsam, so the title remained.

The harbour air was sticky, laden with the odour of shells dumped outside tall, black-timbered whelk cabins and Pearl's mind travelled back to the death of a local fisherman – an old friend of the Nolan family and the supplier of Pearl's oysters – whose body Pearl had discovered on the eve of the oyster festival, out at sea, entangled in the anchor chain of his boat. It hardly seemed possible that such gruesome events could occur in what was now known as a pleasant holiday destination. Increasingly, though, it appeared to Pearl that, from time to time, a stone would be tossed into Whitstable's ostensibly calm estuary waters, the ripples from which would eddy throughout the whole town. The stone was murder, and Pearl knew it was impossible to escape its dark consequences.

'Can I ask what brought you to Whitstable?' she asked.

Natasha seemed momentarily caught out by Pearl's question but she replied: 'It was time for a change of scenery and routine.' She looked out to sea. 'Vic and I met in London and lived in Kensington for almost a decade. We were both ready for something quite different. Simple pleasures, like waking up to church bells or the sound of breaking waves last thing at night. It feels good to be on the edge of the sea – instead of a sea of people . . . Now we have our lovely cottage on the coast.'

'And a gallery in Harbour Street,' said Pearl.

'Victor needs to keep busy. But he's still close enough to London for business. Art is his life.' She sipped her coffee.

'But not yours?'

Natasha stared towards a group of passengers who were boarding an old Thames sailing barge named *Greta* for a voyage around the bay. 'I'm afraid I haven't done much with my life,' she confessed, 'other than marrying Vic. I'm happy to be a support to him. He's a wonderful man. He works very hard.'

'And you love him,' said Pearl.

'But of course,' Vanessa replied.

'And Caroline used to represent you?'

'Victor,' said Natasha. 'The art world can be very closed – cliquey – but Caro opened doors for Vic's customers. The London gallery came alive because she was so full of ideas about how to promote it. Caro always knew how to make things happen.'

'Including you moving here?'

Natasha looked at Pearl. 'Victor and I both wanted to do this,' she said, still holding Pearl's gaze, as though she felt it was important to make this point. Then she became reflective. 'Sometimes things happen and . . . you realise change is not only possible, it's necessary.'

'And Caroline was the catalyst for change?'

Natasha seemed vaguely wounded, as though she was unsure of Pearl's reason for asking. 'Yes,' she finally agreed. 'You could say that.'

Pearl finished her tea and tossed the beaker into a bin. 'Franco told me it was Caroline who found your cottage for you, as well as letting Victor know about the gallery space.'

'That's true,' said Natasha. 'She was an incredible lady. Formidable. Tenacious too. It's almost impossible to believe she's no longer here.' She rubbed her brow, then suddenly turned to Pearl. 'You know Franco is broken-hearted. He really needs you to find the killer. But how can you? The police don't seem to have any leads at all.'

Pearl decided to confide: 'It's been suggested that David Chappell may have been the one person with the most to lose.'

Natasha hesitated. Then: 'From that notice he received, you mean? I'm sure that wasn't Caro's doing. She said she knew nothing about it. Franco believes she was telling the truth – and so do I . . . I don't know this man Chappell but, well, he does seem rather unstable at the moment, with relationship problems.'

'His marriage ended,' Pearl explained. 'His wife left him for another man.'

'Oh, I'm sorry,' said Natasha, seeming to recoil, as though Pearl had touched a nerve. 'Well . . . I suppose we can't help loving who we love. And while I'm sure it's painful for him right now . . . if two people are meant to be together, nothing can stop that.' She seemed to struggle, then went on: 'Hopefully one day he'll find a way to forgive her and move on.' She looked at Pearl plaintively, as though needing approval.

Pearl found it hard to do anything other than give it. 'Yes,' she said finally. 'Hopefully, he will.'

After her conversation with Natasha Bessant, Pearl arrived home to her empty cottage. Unexpectedly, Natasha had offered her food for thought – not so much about Caroline's murder but about life in general and the inevitable need for change. Tossing her keys onto the sofa, she went upstairs and opened the door to Charlie's room, remembering the sharp pang of loss she had suffered a few years ago when her son had left home for college. Those years had flown by, broken into manageable term-sized chunks, and although Charlie had lived away from home for much of the time since then, his old room was always there for him. There had been many occasions when Pearl had commanded him to tidy it but now she missed seeing Charlie's clothes strewn around – welcome evidence of his presence in the cottage.

The room had been Pearl's as a child – kept orderly in a reaction against Dolly's natural tendency to create and tolerate chaos. But once it had become Charlie's territory, Pearl had decorated the walls with baby transfers, then cartoon characters, toddler graffiti overlaid in time with posters of film and pop stars and images of famous models until, as a teenager, Charlie had painted the walls matt black, and hung reproductions of his favourite art – Mondrian, Klee and Bridget Riley. It was a final assertion of independence and an indication of the direction his future studies would take when he had accepted places at university to study, first, history of art and latterly graphics. Since that time, he had struggled to find secure long-term employment but had relied on the restaurant to provide some income when he had been able to wait on tables at The Whitstable Pearl, never straying beyond Kent for long. Now Pearl realised his new relationship might take him away from Whitstable for good.

For a moment she allowed herself to imagine what this room might look like if all evidence of her son disappeared. Perhaps it could become an office space for

McGuire. If they were finally to marry, it would make sense for them to live at Seaspray Cottage – the family home in which Pearl had grown up and which her parents had occupied since their marriage. Pearl's father, Tommy, had died when Pearl was a teenager, having spent a lifetime dredging for oysters, a life misspent, some would say, since Tommy Nolan had been, at heart, a poet, who had instilled a love of poetry in his daughter. As a young man he had charmed the customers of seafront bars with his own verses set to music, wistful lines employing metaphors about life, love and fishing for oysters, before marrying Dolly – who hated them.

Memories lingered for Pearl in every room of the cottage – benign ghosts from the past, always ready to provide reassurance whenever she turned to them. She closed her eyes and saw her father heading home on his boat after a fishing trip and imagined herself as a child, waiting on the harbour arm to welcome him home.

Decades later, once the restaurant had provided financial security, Pearl had taken out a mortgage on the previously rented cottage, intent on keeping hold of the secure home in which she had brought up her own child, while Dolly had moved to Harbour Street. Opening her eyes once more, Pearl stared out of the window to see no fishing boats heading home, only jet skis ploughing waves in the estuary water. No fishing boats. No Tommy Nolan. And soon, perhaps, no Charlie. Change was due and could no longer be ignored just as Natasha Bessant had said only an hour ago.

As she thought about this, Pearl was distracted by her phone ringing. It was McGuire. 'Russ Parker.'

'What about him?' said Pearl, leaving Charlie's room to go downstairs.

'He may be a good roofer but he's a poor businessman.' McGuire paused. 'He's also got a taste for the high life.'

'Marbella?' said Pearl, moving through her living room into the kitchen to take a bottle of Pinot Grigio from the fridge.

'Out of his league,' said McGuire. 'He may have spun his new squeeze a story about making a life there, but he has a county court judgment against him that won't expire for another two years, so his credit record is compromised.'

Pearl sipped the chilled wine she had just poured. 'Love and money . . .' she said softly, thinking about this.

'Sorry?' said McGuire.

'It doesn't matter,' she said. 'Thanks for finding this out.'

'No problem,' said McGuire. 'But that's not all I managed to dig up.'

'Oh?'

'Your chicken lady . . .'

'Vanessa?'

'She has a history of violence.'

Pearl smiled. 'I think you're mistaken.'

'No mistake,' said McGuire. 'Did you know she used to belong to an animal rights group?'

Pearl set down her glass. 'No, I didn't.'

McGuire spoke quickly. 'She was arrested after attacking a lorry driver involved in live-animal export at the port of Ramsgate.'

Pearl tried to summon up an image of Vanessa engaged in one of the angry protests that Pearl knew had taken place at the port for decades. 'Are you absolutely sure?' she asked. 'I find it hard to believe that Vanessa has any kind of record because this would surely have impacted her working in a nursery.'

'She was only seventeen at the time,' said McGuire, 'so the offence was dealt with by a youth court . . . It might have taken place a while ago, Pearl. But it still shows what she's capable of.'

CHAPTER TWENTY-THREE

'I must say, it was very nice of you to cook for us like this,' said Madge Tolliday, setting her knife and fork together on an empty plate at The Whitstable Pearl.

'It was a pleasure, Madge,' said Pearl, as Ruby took away the plate.

'Nothing like a kipper for breakfast,' added Madge.

'Brunch,' said Dolly. 'And it was an Arbroath smokie.'

Madge looked confused so Pearl explained: 'Kippers are cold-smoked herrings, but smokies are haddock and hot-smoked.'

Ted tipped his head towards Madge. 'Coming from Stepney, Madge is more used to jellied eels, aren't you?'

Madge smiled at the thought. 'I must admit I do love a bit of pie and mash with a few hot eels and liquor.'

Pearl leaned in to Ted. 'And how were your Eggs Benedict?'

'Very special,' Ted replied. 'Excellent eggs, Pearl.' He dabbed his mouth with a napkin.

'They were from Vanessa's hens,' Pearl explained. 'Her two remaining girls are now laying as usual, undisturbed by all that's happened lately.'

'If only they could tell us what they might have seen on that allotment,' Dolly commented ruefully.

Ted and Madge shared a look.

'I had no idea you were there, that night, Ted, when I arrived to deal with the composter,' said Pearl.

'And found Caroline Lanzi's body,' said Dolly.

'Why did you take off like that?' Pearl asked him.

'Well,' said Ted, 'I happened to hear someone coming, and as I wasn't planning on staying long, I just didn't want to get involved. Although,' he added quickly, 'if I'd known it was you, Pearl, I'd have stayed to say hello. But I was only there to pick up my specs, and once I'd done that, I headed off home again along the embankment.'

'And you didn't see anyone else there that evening?' asked Pearl.

Ted shook his head. 'I was only there for a few minutes. I'd left my glasses by the hive.'

'So he picked 'em up and made a *beeline* back home.' Madge giggled.

'But you didn't tell the police you'd been there,' said Pearl.

Ted gave her a guilty look. 'No. When they took me in after that telly appeal, I told them I'd forgotten, got confused but, to be honest, once I'd heard that Mrs L had been murdered, I thought it was best to keep schtum.'

'Or else he'd be in the frame for murder,' said Madge, in a hushed whisper.

Ted turned to her. 'You watch too many police shows.'

'I like 'em,' said Madge, 'especially the whodunits.' She looked a little unsure now. 'Not that I guess many of them right, these days. I keep forgetting who did what and when.'

'You're not the only one,' said Dolly. 'It gets harder for us all to keep up as we get older.'

Ted reached into his jacket for his wallet. 'You really should let us pay for our breakfast, Pearl.'

'Brunch!' said Madge.

'It's on the house, Ted. I insist,' said Pearl.

Madge smiled. 'Thank you, Pearl. That's much appreciated. Ted has been through a right ordeal with this wrongful arrest.' She turned to him. 'Got everything? Remember your checklist? Spectacles, testicles . . .'

'Wallet and watch,' said Ted, giving a salute. 'All present and correct!'

Madge returned his smile and the pair began to move off together. At the door they waved, and once they had left, Pearl and Dolly watched them through the restaurant window as they disappeared along the high street.

'Nice they've got each other to rely on,' said Dolly.

'Yes,' Pearl agreed, 'but I can't help thinking there's something not quite right about—'

Before she could go on, Ruby called to her from the kitchen door. Moving quickly to her, Pearl saw she was clutching the restaurant's cordless phone. She offered it to Pearl. 'For you.'

Pearl was surprised to hear Florence Brightling's voice on the line. 'I'm so sorry to bother you,' Florence began. 'I realise you'll be busy with the restaurant at the moment, but I wonder if we could possibly meet up later?'

'What is it?' asked Pearl, noting Florence's anxious tone.

'It's a bit difficult for me to explain now,' the young woman began, 'but is there any chance you could come over to the cottage later, at five? Joe said he's going for a walk then and it'll be easier for me to explain without him here.'

'Of course,' said Pearl, before she thought to ask: 'Is everything all right, Florence?'

'Yes. Or, rather, I'm sure it will be, once I've spoken to you.'

Later that day, after finishing at the restaurant, Pearl picked up a few items of shopping in the high street, then took a shortcut through one of the town's many alleys to the beach. She felt the need to clear the cobwebs from her mind and being close to the sea always helped, but arriving on the beach, west of Seaspray Cottage, she found the tide was out. She stopped to take stock of a group of four-storey houses at a parade called Wave Crest, recalling that at least one of the current owners had bought two neighbouring houses to create an even larger, more impressive home. Beyond this, a pretty row of colourful cottages at Marine Terrace soon came into view, which never failed to capture the attention of inquisitive tourists in the summer months. Visitors were apt to peer through the front windows as they also tried to do while passing Pearl's back garden, and she was reminded that the Bessants had commented on this at the meeting Caroline Lanzi had called. Still thinking about this, Pearl walked beyond Seaspray Cottage and went to stand on the beach at the sea side of the Bessants' new home.

The cottage had once been a fishermen's pub that had thrived in the heyday of the oyster industry. At that time, scores of pubs had existed along Whitstable's coast with many later converted to dwellings. The Bessants' home had become a modest cottage but had since been extended. An old painted wooden balcony that had once weathered decades of sea spray and high winds had been replaced with transparent glass panels, while the garden, previously filled with coast-hardy perennials like agapanthus, euphorbia and veronica, was landscaped with turf and bordered only with yucca and cordyline. Bi-fold doors had replaced a set of Provençal shutters – all now lined with beige blinds to keep out prying eyes. The Bessants' Island Wall home resembled so many of the seaside residences that now belonged to newly settled DFLs. In spite of all Pearl had learned from Natasha about the couple's need for change, she found it hard to believe that the same need might not arise again, prompting the Bessants to move on in due course – as so many DFLs were apt to do. More would simply take their place.

Returning to Seaspray Cottage, Pearl opened her garden gate and negotiated her way down the steps to her beach-hut office, framed with billowing clouds of lavender. As she rounded the structure, she stopped dead in her tracks to see McGuire seated on the patio, a carafe of white wine in his hand. She began to walk towards him – and an unexpected banquet on the table: a seafood quiche, a green salad and a platter of fresh asparagus. Her mouth dropped open. 'You *made* this?'

'If I had,' said McGuire, 'it would have been beans on toast. The quiche won't be a patch on yours – I had it delivered from that new restaurant in the harbour. We missed having supper due to the murder so I thought we could try again.' He offered her a glass of wine.

Pearl sipped and held his gaze as she leaned in to kiss him. 'Thank you.'

McGuire settled back in his chair, relieved Pearl was pleased with his surprise. As a police detective, he was used to noticing small details, storing them in his memory in case he should need to relate them for a court appearance or to reconstruct a Photo-fit likeness. It was an essential part of his job. But now, as Pearl began serving the salad, he took some time to absorb every detail of her appearance – simply for pleasure. After she had handed him his plate, McGuire asked: 'What're you thinking?'

She sat down and unfolded a napkin. 'That I can't wait for you to be properly back on your feet.' She took a sip of her wine and nodded towards the coastline. 'You've never been sailing with me because something's always got in the way. Usually work.'

McGuire gave a casual shrug. 'I'm a landlubber, Pearl. You know that. And what usually gets in the way is murder.' He added: 'Maybe if we agree not to let that happen we could keep things on an even keel.' He raised a smile at the nautical metaphor. As a London man who had fallen for the daughter of an oyster fisherman he knew little about the sea. Nevertheless, with each passing day he spent with Pearl, he felt the city seeping out of his system.

Pearl noted the twinkle in his eye. 'I could show you the ropes,' she smiled at her own figure of speech, 'but a boat has only one captain. Do you always need to be the one in control?' She sipped her wine as she waited for his response.

McGuire met her gaze, becoming more serious now. 'No,' he replied. 'But I don't like being in competition with you.'

Brought up short by his response, Pearl frowned. 'Is that how you think it is?'

McGuire thought carefully before replying. 'That's how it feels sometimes.'

Pearl set down her glass. 'Okay,' she said. 'It's good that you're being honest with me because I feel some resentment about your relationship with Bates.'

'There *is* no relationship,' said McGuire.

'Your working relationship,' Pearl clarified. 'You sit down together, share information. You respect what she does—'

'She's a police sergeant,' McGuire broke in.

'And I'm your partner,' said Pearl, calmly, as she picked up her glass again.

'That's right,' McGuire agreed, 'but not my partner in crime.' He tried to gather his thoughts, aware that the one thing he could be absolutely sure about in that moment was that he and Pearl were opposites. She was a family person; he was a sociable loner. She was for instinct; he trusted procedure. She was small-town; he was city. But she would always be an amateur detective while McGuire was an experienced professional who lived for his job. And nothing could change that. 'Look, the only thing that's ever come between us is—' Again he broke off, reluctant to upset her.

'What?' asked Pearl.

McGuire registered her need to know and set down his fork. 'We've been here before, Pearl. You think you need to prove yourself, but you don't. You've proved yourself to me and everyone else over and over again. You're a good PI. You can read people, and you know your community here, so you've solved homicides and you've helped me to do the same. You've shown just about everyone that you would have made a great cop. But you're not a cop. You're Pearl Nolan. You have a restaurant, a family and friends. You're more than enough for everyone, Pearl, but maybe we're not enough for you.'

Pearl appeared stung, but gave careful thought to all that he had just said. Then: 'Look, I know that, like Charlie, you don't want me doing this. You'd rather I just run the restaurant and stayed at home. Stopped getting involved. Closed the agency and left things to you. But I can no more do that than you could leave things to Hale – and that's not because I think I'm better than you, and not because I want to compete but because I know that together you and I make a perfect team.'

'And is that all we are? A "team"?'

Pearl scanned his blue eyes. 'No,' she said softly, 'we're much more.' She moved closer now and kissed him, and in that moment all the tension she had been feeling began to melt, like the waves on the foreshore – until she suddenly pulled away.

'What is it?' asked McGuire, alarmed.

'Florence!' said Pearl. 'I said I'd go and see her.' She checked her watch.

McGuire frowned. 'What about?'

'I don't know – yet.' She jumped to her feet but McGuire laid a hand on hers. 'Tell her you can't make it.'

Pearl looked at him. 'I can't,' she said truthfully. 'I know where she lives but I don't have her number.'

'Pearl?'

She read the look in his eyes but still felt the need to assert herself. 'I'm late,' she explained. 'And I said I'd be there so I really have to go.' She grabbed her bag and hurried down the garden path while McGuire stared after her. As she disappeared along the promenade, he glanced at the abandoned meal and knocked back his glass of wine.

*

Just over ten minutes later, Pearl's Fiat drew up at the cottage shared by Joe Fuller and Florence Brightling. Set back on an unadopted road, the old property was part of an area that was still referred to by local people as Brooklands Farm, but which, centuries ago, had been natural woodland. Like so much of Whitstable, it was now under threat from encroaching building developments. At one point it had provided some of the finest and most versatile agricultural land in the area, and though some parts were still used for cereal crops, much of it had already disappeared. What could still be enjoyed was the green valley of Swalecliffe Brook, which continued to offer rural tranquillity to walkers, undisturbed by much, other than the wind blowing through the trees and the rippling of the brook. In this peaceful setting, Joe and Florence's cottage stood alone, a remnant of the past.

Pearl headed up an old York stone path to the front door, which was shaded by a wooden porch Joe had crafted. The couple's home was quaint but there was also a hint of rebellion in its celebration of the past, evident in Joe's use of old materials and his mastery of the ancient art of wood carving. Pearl was reminded of Dolly's comment about Joe Fuller's work being distinct from what Victor Bessant usually showcased, but perhaps it was true that Victor had recognised its intrinsic and financial value – or had at least been persuaded of both by Natasha. If so, then Mrs Bessant was certainly more than the attractive trophy wife Dolly had first taken her for.

It was also true that Caroline Lanzi's death had somehow created an outcome that had proved beneficial to Joe and Florence – and might yet create more financial security for them with a wider appreciation of Joe's work. Pearl knocked on the cottage door and waited for a response. Silence. She knocked again, but still no one answered. Checking her watch, Pearl saw it was now almost five thirty. She felt disappointed with herself for having forgotten the appointment, while blaming McGuire in part for having distracted her with his surprise lunch – and confounding her with all the points he had raised. McGuire had never hidden his concerns about Pearl's involvement in local crime but what was the point of repeating them yet again? He must know that she would resent having to tell Franco Lanzi that he must rely solely on DI Hale's investigation into his wife's murder. Pearl felt she could no more do that than relieve herself of the responsibility to apologise to Florence for missing their appointment.

She was about to return to her car when her attention was drawn to the cottage's front window. A tabby kitten was mewing silently on the other side of the pane, scraping a paw down the glass. Pearl moved closer, meeting the paw with her finger on the window. The kitten wiped its head against the pane as if in need of company and Pearl leaned closer, shading her eyes as she tried to peer through into the living room. She found herself unable to see much beyond the kitten. Remembering that Florence had said she didn't like to leave Floss alone for long,

Pearl decided to investigate the rear of the cottage in case Florence was there. Beyond an unlocked wooden gate, Pearl found only a pretty courtyard garden and an open kitchen door swinging on its hinges in the warm breeze. She called to Florence but, only silence followed. Pearl decided to enter.

In the kitchen, she was met with an old-fashioned clothes rail laden with Joe's shirts. A heavy pine table was still set for breakfast: muesli, marmalade and a jar of Ted Rowden's illicit Whitstable Honey. A wooden box containing some of Joe's carving tools had been left on a window seat. On the ring of a gas stove, a large saucepan was simmering beneath a lit flame. Pearl called again – louder this time: 'Florence?'

She moved to the cooker and saw water bubbling in the bottom of the pan while a colander of scrubbed vegetables stood in the butler sink. Turning the gas off, Pearl went into the hallway where she could hear the kitten mewing. A ball of tabby fur scurried towards her, the kitten winding its tiny body around her ankles as though grateful for company. Pearl picked up Florence Brightling's new pet, gave the little creature a kiss, and noticed that the door to the middle room of the cottage was closed. Pearl tapped on it, then opened it to see an old wooden rocking chair facing a window. Florence's fair hair was falling over one arm of the rocker, her head tilted towards the door, eyes closed. Pearl held her breath, bracing herself as she reached out to touch Florence's shoulder. Immediately the young woman's china-blue eyes opened and a sleepy smile crept across her face. 'Pearl . . .'

Relieved, Pearl explained: 'I knocked on the door and called but . . .'

'I'm so sorry,' said Florence, gathering her senses. 'I haven't been sleeping too well lately. I just sat down for a moment and must have dropped off. I thought you weren't coming.'

'I'm late,' Pearl confirmed, 'and I'm sorry about that, but something came up. You said you wanted to talk?'

Florence nodded and got up. Smiling, she took the kitten from Pearl and led the way back to the kitchen. 'What I said the other night,' she began, indicating for Pearl to take a seat at the table, 'Joe was right to stop me.' She took some cat food from the fridge and emptied it into a saucer for the kitten, then joined Pearl. 'I really shouldn't have been going on like that to you.' She paused. 'After all, someone has lost their life . . . and there I was, telling you how wonderful it was that some of Joe's work has sold.'

'Well,' began Pearl, 'you were right that it was a welcome piece of news among the tragedy. And you have every right to be pleased about it.'

Florence still appeared conflicted. 'I know. And it really has been very difficult, especially for Joe.'

'Losing his workshop, you mean?'

Florence nodded. 'Without it he hasn't been able to work, you see, so I've been keeping us afloat, using money left to me by an aunt. Joe hates being dependent on me

– he said I'm his muse, not his mother.' She smiled sadly. 'I kept telling him not to worry, and that something would come up, that our luck would finally change, but that's why the complaint to the council was such a blow. I don't think I've ever seen Joe so angry. He wanted to have it out with Caroline straight after that meeting. He said the least she could do was own up to making all those complaints. I managed to stop him. I distracted him by persuading him to sort out all his tools. He's still got a lot stored here at home.' She gestured to the box on the window seat.

'That was a good thing to do,' said Pearl.

'Yes. He was even talking about selling them all, but I've never doubted that Joe's work was good enough for him to succeed, and this opportunity at the gallery has given him the confidence to continue. He's like a changed man.'

'So what's the problem?'

'Well . . .' said Florence '. . . it's not a problem, as such, it's just—' She broke off as she met Pearl's gaze, then glanced again towards Joe's tools. 'I just wanted you to know, that's all.'

Pearl was confused. There was nothing seemingly important or urgent in what Florence had just relayed but the visit had taken Pearl away from McGuire. She had deserted him to sit across a kitchen table from Florence Brightling, who still resembled an anxious child in spite of what she had just imparted. Pearl wondered if the reversal of the couple's usual roles, as provider and dependant, had actually caused more problems in their relationship than Florence had just owned up to.

But before she could enquire further, a knock on the front door sounded and Florence excused herself to answer it. Pearl hoped it might just be Joe, and that a chance to observe the couple together might give her a better idea of Florence's concerns. But from the hallway she heard a few voices before the kitchen door opened and Florence came in, two uniformed police officers following her. 'I'm sorry, Pearl,' she began. 'They say they're here for you.'

CHAPTER TWENTY-FOUR

D I Hale sat across from Pearl in an interview room at Canterbury CID, a tape machine on the table that separated them, monitored by a young detective sergeant. Hale fixed Pearl with a hard stare.

'Well,' she responded casually, 'are you going to tell me what this is about?' She glanced towards the young man beside Hale. 'I don't even know the name of your officer here.'

'DS Akhtar,' said the young man, helpfully, offering Pearl the faintest of smiles.

Pearl returned it while Hale, observing this with clear displeasure, scowled. 'Now we've got the pleasantries over, perhaps we could make a start.'

Akhtar looked chastened while Hale gave his attention to some paperwork before him. 'Care to tell me why you went to the home of Joe Fuller and Florence Brightling this afternoon?'

Pearl shrugged. 'Florence called me this morning and asked me to pop round.'

'Why?'

'Because she wanted to discuss something.'

'Discuss what?'

'Recent events,' said Pearl.

'You mean,' said Hale, 'the murder of Caroline Lanzi?'

'No,' Pearl replied. 'The sale of Joe's work.'

Hale frowned but Pearl smiled. 'If you didn't know, Joe's a wood sculptor. And a very good one too.'

Hale's eyes narrowed. 'And this wasn't something you could've discussed the other night?'

Pearl allowed Hale's question to hang.

'You had a meeting with the allotment holders,' Hale went on. 'At your home. And I'm guessing that wasn't about turnips.' He kept his eyes fixed on Pearl as he leaned towards the recorder: 'For the benefit of the tape Ms Nolan is—'

Pearl spoke over him. 'Yes,' she said sharply. 'I did invite the allotment holders to my home . . . And I take it you've got me under surveillance now?'

Hale said nothing.

She leaned forward in her chair. 'Why?'

Hale swallowed hard as though holding down a decision not to reply. Pearl persisted. 'Are you tracking my car?' she asked. 'Intercepting my email correspondence, my texts?'

He continued to stare at her – mute.

'Well?' she demanded, increasingly frustrated.

'You have a habit of becoming involved in murder,' Hale announced.

'But I'm no murderer,' said Pearl, a curious smile now forming on her lips. 'In fact, I'm as innocent as Ted Rowden.'

Hale looked at her with suspicion. 'Why do you mention Rowden?'

Pearl shrugged and sat back. 'You had to let him go in spite of two eye-witness reports placing him on the embankment near the allotment just before I found Caroline Lanzi's body.'

'Why d'you think he was there?' asked Hale.

Pearl stared at the barred window. 'He told me he'd left his glasses there and that he'd returned to his plot to fetch them but he got confused about the time.'

'And do you believe him?' asked Hale.

'Do you?' said Pearl.

Hale didn't reply.

Pearl went on: 'I've known Ted Rowden for a very long time and I've *never* known him to be violent. He's a beekeeper and a gardener. He spends a lot of time at the allotment and it's more than possible that he left his glasses there, then went back to pick them up and forgot about it. All the same,' she went on, 'it was a good call on your part to stage that TV appeal.' She paused. 'Just a shame it didn't produce any results other than an eighty-year-old man having forgotten his specs.'

At this, Hale's lips tightened before he met Pearl's gaze. 'I'll remind you, Ms Nolan, to continue to make yourself available for questioning. That means staying in Whitstable and cooperating fully with my enquiries.'

'I've no intention of going anywhere else,' said Pearl, smoothly.

'That's good. Especially as my own enquiries, so far, lead me to believe that you happen to be in a relationship with a senior member of this department who is *not* assigned to this case but *has* been requesting information concerning it.'

Pearl recognised the need to protect McGuire. 'I have a right to privacy . . . and protection against unnecessary intrusion into my private life.'

'Your human rights?' Hale scoffed. 'I think you'll find those are trumped by *my* rights as a police officer involved in the prevention or detection of a serious crime.' He sat back in his seat and watched her. 'You may enjoy playing private eye, Ms Nolan. You may even have fancied yourself as a police officer, but from where I'm sitting, you're just a small-town busybody getting in the way of a serious crime investigation. Is that clear?'

'Perfectly.'

Hale nodded to Akhtar but as the DS made a move to the tape machine, Pearl spoke again. 'I haven't quite finished,' she went on, 'but for the benefit of the tape, I'd like to remind *you*, DI Hale, that this crime took place in my home town – and the husband of the murder victim has charged *me* to find the killer. While I won't be leaving Whitstable, I *will* continue to do just that, especially considering your lack of progress so far.'

She faced him down. Hale waved a hand to Akhtar, who got the message and terminated the recording.

It was almost sunset by the time Pearl returned to Whitstable. Before heading back to Seaspray Cottage, she checked her phone and called Dolly, who answered quickly: 'Where are you? Florence said you'd been picked up by the police.'

'They released me. I'm down on the beach, heading home.'

'Have they finished with you?'

Pearl sighed. 'Yes. And I with them, in more ways than one.' Troubled, she added, 'Look, I haven't been able to get through to—'

'Mike?' said Dolly.

'Yes,' said Pearl. 'I've tried him but he hasn't called me.'

Dolly spoke over her. 'He had to go to hospital, Pearl.'

Brought up short, Pearl was silenced briefly. 'Why?' she asked, in a shocked whisper.

'Because—'

Before Dolly could go on, Pearl lowered her phone as she heard someone call her name. Turning, she saw McGuire a few metres away on the beach. He was standing close to the shore, and came slowly towards her. As he did so Pearl realised something important and ended the call to Dolly.

'The cast . . .'

McGuire spoke: 'It's gone.'

'For good?'

'No more Long John Silver.' McGuire opened his arms wide and Pearl took a step forward, allowing him to hold her tight, her eyes closed, pleased not to be seeing DI Hale's smirking face. When they broke apart, she asked: 'Can we go for a walk?'

McGuire offered her his arm. Pearl took it.

It didn't take long for Pearl and McGuire to find a quiet spot on the north side of the harbour. Pearl indicated a carved wooden bench that faced out to sea. McGuire sat down and she joined him. He looked pensive, weighing up all she had just explained to him. 'Do you think Hale could cause trouble for you?' she asked.

McGuire met her gaze. 'He'll try,' he said, 'and Welch will be more than ready to listen.'

Pearl sighed. 'Well, at least you're out of plaster now. Why didn't you tell me about the hospital appointment?'

'I thought it would make a nice surprise – like the meal?'

'It did,' she said, 'especially after everything else. Shame my visit to Florence spoiled it.'

'And what was it she wanted to see you about?'

'I'm not sure. The police intervened.' She turned to McGuire. 'I think she may just have wanted to offload the problems she and Joe had been having. They've always been so close. Inseparable. They've been together since they were teenagers and it's almost impossible to think of them as separate individuals.'

'Until recently,' said McGuire. 'You said things are changing for Joe. Maybe he wants to move on, leave Florence behind?'

Pearl shook her head. 'I can't imagine that . . .' She trailed off.

McGuire took up the thread. 'No one really knows what goes on between two people behind closed doors.'

'That's true,' said Pearl, recalling that Dolly had said the same, referring to David and Cindy Chappell.

McGuire noted Pearl's preoccupation and took advantage of it. 'Maybe it's best to leave it to Hale.'

'You surely can't mean that?'

'He's taken Bates off the case, Pearl. I've lost my source. Hale's privy to all the forensics, evidence we won't have access to. Maybe he'll even stage another appeal.'

'And come up with another wrong conclusion.' She got to her feet and paced in frustration. '*So* many times I've thought that the answer is here *somewhere* – among everything that's happened, everything that was said. But I just can't find the key to it.'

She looked away, as if for inspiration, and noticed an ice-cream van parked at the harbour. A queue of customers had formed. At the head, she saw Russ Parker handing a cornet to Cindy, slipping his arm around her shoulders as they moved off together.

'There's two people who look like they haven't a care in the world,' murmured McGuire.

'Yes,' Pearl agreed, 'they're happy, even though it's only ice cream they're enjoying.'

'And not champagne?'

Pearl kept her eyes on the couple as they stood close together near the lifeboat station's slipway, gazing out to sea where a dinghy race was taking place. 'Russ has always been one for the high life, big ambitions . . .'

'Even bigger debts?' said McGuire.

Pearl considered this. 'He's flashy, but no murderer, I'm sure of that.'

'Instinct?'

Pearl inclined her head.

'And you haven't changed your mind about Natasha and Franco?'

'I had a coffee with her yesterday and I understood what she was trying to explain to me about the need for change.' She looked at McGuire. 'You acted on that yourself when you decided not to go back to London.'

McGuire held her gaze. 'I couldn't do anything but stay.'

'I'm glad you did.'

They shared a smile and Pearl found herself stroking the intricate carving on the bench, thinking of a box of wood-carving tools sitting on a kitchen window seat.

'You're right that we can't ever know what goes on between two people,' she began, 'but I'm sure Joe and Florence love one another . . . I think the same about Michael and Vanessa.'

'And the Bessants?'

'Victor loves art and Natasha loves Victor.'

'And Franco?'

For a moment Pearl didn't know how to answer McGuire's question, then said: 'I do believe he loved Caroline.'

McGuire frowned. 'Why? You hardly got to see them together.'

'That's true,' said Pearl, 'but after she died I went to talk to him. He was sitting opposite me on a beautiful white sofa, staring across at me ... I realised he was looking in my direction but trying to see Caroline still sitting there – alive and well. It was a look I won't forget.'

'And now she's dead,' said McGuire, breaking the spell, 'and he'll have her money.'

Pearl watched a small fleet of fishing boats enter the harbour and thought of her father, returning after a day spent dredging for native oysters, more than ready to spoil his daughter with treats paid for by his fishing trip.

'Shall we get an ice cream?' said McGuire.

Pearl turned to him and smiled.

Heading across to the ice-cream van, McGuire put in his order while Pearl hung back to inspect a harbour noticeboard, slipping on her glasses to read a colourful notice advertising the upcoming carnival. She caught sight of a familiar leaflet, one of Russ Parker's, advertising his professional skills, touting for work. Pearl looked back again at where Cindy and Russ had been standing near the lifeboat station's slipway – but saw they were no longer there. As an elderly couple passed by on a pair of mobility scooters, a thought came to Pearl. 'Of course . . .' she said softly to herself, as McGuire returned with two ice-cream cones. 'You were right all along!' she exclaimed.

McGuire looked puzzled. 'Right about what?'

Pearl grabbed the ice-cream cones and dumped them in a bin. 'We need to act – now!'

CHAPTER TWENTY-FIVE

Night had just fallen as Pearl locked the front door to The Whitstable Pearl. Her guests took their places at the tables, and Victor Bessant asked: 'What on earth are we doing here?'

Sitting on Victor's right side, Natasha laid a gentle hand on her husband's forearm, then raised a comforting smile for Franco, who was sitting on her left.

Cindy Chappell commented from the other side of the room: 'For a minute I thought we were being invited for that supper you promised us, Pearl.' She glanced at Russ Parker beside her, only to see his stony expression.

'Not tonight, Cindy,' said Pearl.

Russ threw a look across the room to David Chappell. 'Well, whatever this is about, you should think about getting the police here in case *he* kicks off.'

'And is that what you'd like?' asked Pearl.

Russ shrugged. 'I'm just saying – there's no guarantee that he won't.'

David Chappell eyed his rival but before he could respond Michael Stopes asked Pearl: 'What *is* this about?'

Pearl paused, then took a deep breath. 'In two words, love and money – or, as someone recently reminded me, the most common motives for murder.'

She cast her eyes around and allowed her gaze to settle on Cindy and her new partner. Russ Parker reacted to Pearl's scrutiny and spoke up. 'You're not suggesting *we* had anything to do with Caroline's murder?'

'You know that's not possible, Pearl,' said Cindy.

'Of course,' Pearl agreed. 'So it was important for me to look elsewhere.' She turned to Joe Fuller, sitting with Florence. 'Especially to anyone who might have benefited from Caroline Lanzi's murder, even indirectly, by us all being brought together.'

Joe shook his head slowly in disbelief. 'Why are you looking at me?' he asked. Florence took his hand.

Pearl went on softly, 'It was only after Caroline's death that things began to come together for you, Joe, for your work to begin selling at The Front . . . and all because you'd become better acquainted with Natasha and Victor.' She paused to frame her thoughts. 'You'd already come into contact with Natasha at the allotment where she'd seen your work as it was being stored in the studio there.'

Florence spoke up. 'I told you that, Pearl. It was no secret.'

Natasha nodded. 'That's right. It was just a coincidence . . . a moment of serendipity. We happened to connect at the right time.'

'And that's something Caroline Lanzi excelled at,' said Pearl, 'making connections. Putting the right people together for mutual benefit.'

Franco spoke up. 'Caroline spent her life doing that. She was good at it,' he said proudly.

Pearl moved closer to him. 'But she was just about to give it all up. Because she had moved here with you, Franco, to begin a new life . . . and you were looking forward to doing all the things you mentioned to me, spending more time together, travelling for fun and not for business – finally being able to enjoy some free time together . . . Caroline may have been giving up her work but you would both have remained financially secure. The only problem was she didn't seem able to give up being herself . . . becoming involved . . . Making things happen?' Pearl moved away from Franco. 'You told me you'd quarrelled after the meeting at your home.' She turned again as she approached a table at which Ted, Madge, Dolly and Marty were all seated together.

'Yes,' said Franco. 'I thought she was wasting her time with these things. Council meetings . . . allotment meetings . . . This idea of hers, the association, would have meant even more meetings. And I saw that she wasn't making friends with all this,' he added. 'Instead she was upsetting people – like she did that night.'

'We were upset because of the complaints,' Madge insisted.

Beside her, Ted nodded. 'That's right, Madge. She didn't have to go running to the council about everyone like that.'

David Chappell spoke. 'Well, we all *assumed* she was the one who'd complained.'

'That's right,' Pearl said. 'From that very first morning when the complaints arrived, when I found you so upset at the allotment, David, after you'd received that council notice, we *all* thought this must have been down to Caroline.'

Marty insisted: '*I* didn't! Like I said from the start, Mrs Lanzi was a lady. I always got on with her.' He gave a nod of solidarity to Franco.

Dolly turned to him. 'And *you* never received a complaint.'

'Because I didn't do anything wrong!' said Marty. 'Not like you lot.'

'There's nothing wrong with keeping bees,' said Ted. 'And the complaint I received was about keeping bees. *Nothing* more.'

'That's right,' said Pearl. 'Nothing more. And the same was true of every other complaint. They were about nothing more than was evident on the site. Your bees, Ted. Your grass and pond, Madge. Vanessa's hens.'

Vanessa added: 'Your lovely chimes, Michael.'

Dolly frowned. '*My* mural.'

Pearl turned to Joe. '*Your* work,' she said, 'which Natasha had seen you bringing into your allotment studio one day.'

Natasha frowned. 'You're not suggesting *I* put in the complaints?'

'*You* didn't get any either,' Madge said, with suspicion.

Victor replied wearily: 'That's because, like Marty, we didn't infringe any regulations.' He rubbed his brow in frustration and turned impatiently to Pearl. 'Look,' he began, 'I came here tonight because I hoped you might finally know more about who committed this murder.'

'And that's *precisely* why I asked you all here,' said Pearl.

David spoke in a hushed whisper. 'You mean you know?'

'Pearl?' said Dolly, unsure.

Pearl took her time to reply. 'One person in this room received the most important complaint – the notice that would have deprived him of his plot, the piece of land that he had begun to hope might help him to recover from the break-up of his marriage.' She turned to David Chappell. 'You have a garden at home, David, and you could have used that as therapy to try to get over your loss. But I'm guessing it must have reminded you too much of Cindy – of the life you shared together, the life you were trying to forget in the bottom of a bottle.'

David looked pained. 'It's true I'd begun drinking,' he admitted, 'but I knew it wasn't the answer. I'd hoped that doing some work at the plot might help. Getting some exercise, restoring some kind of order. Looking forward to a future if only with a crop of plants. That was what I wanted . . . but then the notice came.' His face set. 'And you're right. I was *more* than upset. I was furious about that notice but I *didn't* kill anyone.'

'And you didn't turn up to the meeting either,' said Marty.

'I know,' said David. 'And the simple truth is, I didn't trust myself. Like I say, I was angry.'

'Out of control?' said Pearl.

'No!' David shook his head. 'No, I just wanted to know the truth so I listened from the public path at the end of the garden—'

'Where I found you after the meeting,' said Pearl.

Franco appeared suitably shocked. 'Why didn't you tell me this?' he demanded. 'I hired you to find Caro's killer.'

'Or to make sure you were privy to whatever Pearl or the police discovered,' suggested Dolly.

Before Franco could respond, Victor asked: 'So what *did* they discover? Or is this some kind of game you're playing with us all?'

'If it is, Pearl, please stop,' said Joe.

'It's no game,' Pearl responded, 'though it may have seemed that way to two people here tonight.' She paused again. 'Love and money,' she repeated softly, 'two motives for murder.' She turned to Cindy and Russ. 'You two are clearly very much in love but you're also in need of money.'

Neither spoke so Pearl went on: 'You came back here to Whitstable on the very day Caroline was murdered.'

Cindy nodded. Russ put an arm around her. 'That's right, Pearl. So what?'

'So *why* did you return?' Pearl asked.

Russ frowned. 'Things hadn't gone too well in Spain.'

'Not as well as you'd expected,' said Pearl, 'or perhaps hoped for. A new life together in a new country. Away from Cindy's husband and your creditors, Russ.' She moved closer to Cindy. 'You need a divorce to make a clean break . . .'

Russ caught sight of David's agitation. 'I told you, Pearl,' he warned, pointing to him. 'If you carry on like this you're going to need the police here—'

'In case David "kicks off"?' said Pearl. 'That's the impression you like to give, isn't it? That David is a violent drunk who's incapable of controlling his temper, and who put you in danger, Cindy—'

'That's not true!' David protested. 'I never once harmed you!'

Russ threw up his hands and declared: 'There he goes, *kicking off*! I *warned* you.'

'Love and money,' Pearl repeated. 'Why was Caroline *still* concerning herself with something as mundane as an allotment? Working so hard to form an association, getting embroiled in meetings at the local council and with us, her fellow allotment holders?'

Vanessa asked: 'Why *would* she want to send in those complaints about us?'

'Why indeed?' asked Pearl. 'And why submit them anonymously? When I talked to Councillor Radcliffe about this, he suggested this was to prevent any possible repercussions on the complainant.'

Franco was clearly confused. 'But if the complaints were the motive for her murder,' he began, 'the fact they were anonymous didn't prevent it.'

'Because everyone knew it was her,' said Michael.

'Did we?' queried Pearl. 'I, too, assumed the letters must have been sent by Caroline. She was certainly bold enough to do such a thing to highlight whatever annoyed or irritated her about the site. But several times she denied sending any complaint, and seemed as surprised by them as everyone who received them. She also seemed confused about the questions I asked that night.'

Michael frowned. 'Just her way of trying to excuse herself?'

'Putting us off the scent!' said Madge, giving a nod to Dolly and Ted beside her.

'Perhaps,' said Pearl, 'but the more I found out about Caroline Lanzi, the less likely it seemed to me that she would have hidden behind a cloak of anonymity. As I said, she was bold, and unafraid of repercussions, and the meeting wasn't called to discuss complaints. It was about her new project, the Allotment Association. Nothing else. But we weren't all present at the meeting that evening. One of us failed to come.' She turned to David. 'You admitted you didn't trust yourself. But perhaps you didn't trust how you might react to the one person you had always believed had caused the council to act against you.' Pearl moved closer to him. 'I'd seen how angry you were on receipt of that notice – and though it's true that each of us, apart from Marty and the Bessants, had received a complaint against our regulation breaches, yours was the most important because it threatened the forfeit of your plot. You'd already been warned about your lack of action—'

'When?' interrupted Dolly.

'Thirty days before, almost a month ago, when the council had first written to you and given you that time to respond to the complaint,' said Pearl. 'Thirty days *before* was just around the time that Cindy and Russell had left for Spain.'

'That's right,' said Russ, unabashed.

'Everyone in Whitstable knew when we left,' said Cindy.

'But then you came back,' said Pearl.

Dolly became suspicious. 'And we all thought you'd gone for good.'

'And while David's greatest fear had been that you would never return,' said Pearl, 'you did.' She eyed the couple. 'Why?' She paused. 'Why else? Because it was you two, Cindy and Russ, who submitted those complaints to the council.'

All heads turned to them as Pearl went on. 'A spiteful thing to do, but you'd heard that David had begun drinking after you left him, Cindy, and you hoped that losing his allotment plot would cause him to drink even more, that he'd become unstable, a risk to you, and that would provide you with a good reason in any potential court case resulting from him failing to cooperate with divorce proceedings. Even though it's no longer possible to *contest* a divorce, you still needed David's cooperation *and* his consent to sell the bungalow so you could quickly get your hands on your share of its worth. You believed that if you claimed you had a violent husband with an obvious drink problem you would paint yourself as the victim, which would help your case. When you heard that David was trying to curb his drinking and start work at the allotment, you sent in an anonymous complaint against him to the council. But you couldn't submit only *one* complaint, could you? That might have been too obvious – especially to David.'

Cindy pulled herself up, preparing to defend herself. 'Whatever we might have done with those complaints, we are not murderers!'

'Perhaps not,' said Pearl. She turned back to David. 'I'd witnessed your rage against Caroline, but the idea of love and money, coupled with two eye-witness reports, caused me to suspect someone else.' She turned slowly to Ted Rowden. 'Why did you lie about going to the allotment on the night of Caroline's murder?'

'You know that, Pearl,' remonstrated Dolly.

'He didn't lie,' said Madge. 'He forgot!'

'And then he remembered,' said Pearl. She turned again to him. 'You claimed you needed to go there to pick up your glasses.'

Under Pearl's gaze, Ted remained silent. She went on: 'But you didn't take your mobility scooter there that night. It could well have been spotted on the road or on the parking space by anyone taking a walk near Prospect Field.'

'Ted needed his specs to drive, Pearl!' said Madge in frustration.

'And so he told the police,' said Pearl. 'But today, while I was at the harbour, I happened to remember that Ted had used his mobility scooter on the night of the meeting at Caroline's house ... and he *hadn't* been wearing his glasses. He must have been able to drive without them. And if you *had* left your glasses at the allotment, Ted, you must surely have driven home on your scooter afterwards *without* wearing them? Yet you used that as your excuse to the police for returning to the allotment on foot and making a getaway as soon as I arrived ... *just* before I found Caroline Lanzi's body. Why would you have done that, Ted, if you hadn't been guilty of her murder?'

Pearl fixed him with a hard stare. Ted's lips, already clammed shut, now trembled under her gaze.

CHAPTER TWENTY-SIX

'Well?' said Pearl, still waiting for an answer from Ted Rowden.

Beside him, Madge looked conflicted by her loyalty for her friend and to Pearl's struggle for the truth. Unable to bear this, she cried out: 'Leave him alone!'

But Pearl persisted, softly but insistently: 'Why did you do that, Ted?'

Franco Lanzi pointed an arrow-straight arm at him. 'Because he murdered my wife!'

Joe Fuller looked confounded. 'Is that possible?'

Silence fell. Then Pearl shook her head. 'No,' she said gently. 'Ted was trying to protect someone else.' She looked slowly at Madge and went on: 'You never hid your dislike of Caroline Lanzi, did you, Madge? Or showed any regret that she had been murdered?'

Looking much like an insolent child, Madge blurted: 'Because I didn't feel any.' Her lips pursed. 'Where I come from, we tell it like it is. The woman was arrogant. Selfish.'

Franco looked away sharply, as though he had been slapped.

'So you killed her?' said Natasha in shock.

'Don't be silly!' said Dolly. She turned to Pearl, incredulous. 'You can't possibly think Madge is capable of murder?'

Pearl turned to her mother, but it was Madge who replied, in a helpless whisper: 'I wish I could be sure I wasn't.' She lowered her head.

Michael spluttered, 'What on earth do you mean?'

Ted finally found his voice. 'Leave her alone,' he ordered. Putting an arm around her, he continued: 'Just leave her be.'

A moment passed. Then Pearl asked gently: 'How long has your memory been playing tricks on you, Madge?'

Remaining mute, Dolly's old friend shook her head slowly.

'Stop it,' said Ted, helplessly.

Madge laid a hand on Ted's sleeve before she spoke. 'It's all right, Ted,' she said, suddenly calm. 'Pearl's right. I can't keep it to myself any longer. I have to face up to things.'

Marty seemed bewildered. 'Face up to what?'

Madge was bracing herself to explain. 'Dementia. Alzheimer's? It runs in my family on my mother's side.' She pulled a handkerchief from her sleeve and wiped her eyes before blowing her nose. 'She got it young . . . too young to enjoy the move down here. She was stuck in Stepney all her life – apart from the hop-picking holidays. Magic days . . .' She seemed to drift off for a moment. 'Funny how I can remember all that better than what I did yesterday. But that's how it seems to go. I've always been a bit forgetful – Dolly knows that – but then it started getting worse.' She turned to Ted. 'I was relying on you more and more to remind me of what I had and hadn't done. *And* you, Dolly. Remember after that lift you gave me on the night of the meeting?'

'You'd lost your keys,' said Dolly, pained. 'But then we found them.'

'Yes,' said Madge. 'There's been a lot of that lately.'

Ted patted her hand, then addressed the others: 'I said she should see the doctor. They can give you pills for it, these days.'

'And I did,' said Madge, quickly, 'but then I forgot to take them.' She quietened, as though reliving a difficult memory. 'Then I found myself in Seasalter one night. No idea how I got there but I've always liked it down there because it's nice and peaceful compared to Whitstable.'

'It's a good couple of miles away,' said Dolly.

'That's right,' Madge said, with a smile, then went on: 'The day after we had the meeting, it was so hot . . . I tried to have a nap indoors then got up and went out at some point. Just for some air.' She looked at Ted. 'But it was all a blank after that . . .'

Ted explained: 'She called me. I'm on Madge's phone list. And eventually I found her down the beach near the rock-oyster trestles . . . no shoes on, cuts on her feet. I got her home.' He looked at her. 'You were going on about your pond, how you didn't want the frogs to be without it or the hens to lose their new home.' He glanced at Vanessa and Michael. 'I promised her that wouldn't happen.' Then he turned to Pearl and Dolly. 'But Madge begged me to go to the allotment and check. I said I would so I did. I was going anyway that evening but I didn't take the scooter because I suddenly had an idea . . . After all that bluster from Mrs L about the composter and ordering you to check on it, like she did, Pearl, I decided that if no one was there I'd make sure the ruddy thing was never used again . . . I planned to use that new spading fork to vandalise it,' he confessed unashamedly. 'I thought local yobs would get the blame, not an old-timer like me. Then I'd have got my own back for all the upset caused by those complaints.' He paused.

'It was all quiet when I arrived. No one there. Nothing amiss. I made my way down to the composter and the new fork was right there, but I knew straight away that something was wrong. All the prongs were covered with blood.' Franco closed his eyes but Ted was staring into the distance as he went on: 'I opened the lid of the composter and there she was, Mrs L, lying on top. It looked like someone had used that fork to stab her and she'd fallen back inside and they'd closed the lid.

'Then I thought about Madge. She'd gone missing earlier and she couldn't remember what she'd done. I had this terrible feeling . . .' He looked at everyone in the room. 'I couldn't help a dead woman but I could help Madge. I knew I had to do something. So I emptied a pile of compost out of that trap door on the composter and as everything sank down inside from the top. I forked that compost on top of Mrs L so no one could see. I used to be a grave digger,' he explained. 'Then I washed my hands and was just getting my breath back on the other side of the fence when I heard someone coming.' He looked at Pearl. 'Like I said, I didn't know it was you, Pearl. I just heard footsteps coming closer and I knew I had to take off or I'd be found. So that's what I did – I legged it up the embankment. I didn't know anyone'd seen me – not till the rozzers put that appeal on the telly.' He took a deep breath. 'If I'd only known it was you, Pearl, I would've said something, but in no time the police were on the case, taking statements.'

'So you lied,' said Pearl.

'Because he thought I'd done it!' said Madge. 'I think I may have done it too!'

Franco leaned forward, his elbows on the table, and buried his head in his hands. Natasha tried to comfort him.

'Alzheimer's doesn't make a murderer of you, Madge,' said Dolly.

'Mum's right,' said Pearl. 'What were you thinking, Ted, trying to cover up a murder like this? That's perverting the course of justice.'

Ted gave her a guilty look. 'I know, but . . . I've had a good life, Pearl. And maybe I don't have too much of it left, but if I have to spend the rest of it in an open prison, somewhere there's a bit of gardening to do, it wouldn't be the end of the world, you know?'

Russ Parker looked nonplussed by what he had just heard. 'After that, you'll be lucky if you're not banged up for life in Wormwood Scrubs!'

Madge piped up: 'But he didn't *kill* anyone!'

'And neither did you, Madge,' said Pearl. 'Love and money,' she repeated, urgently now. 'I kept returning to this and began to suspect that two people, other than Cindy and Russ, might also be in need of freeing themselves from their marriages.' She turned to Franco and Natasha.

'*Pura pazzia!*' Franco exclaimed.

'Franco's right,' said Natasha. 'That's madness!'

But Pearl went on: 'I saw you both one morning, talking together near Harbour Street. I knew there was something between you, something that might perhaps provide you both with a motive for murder, but something else kept telling me I was wrong. Why? All I had to go on was . . . instinct. And later, a conversation I had with you, Natasha, when you spoke about forgiveness, about Cindy leaving David for another man? You said we can't help who we fall in love with – which is true – and that you hoped, one day, David might find a way to forgive his wife.'

Pearl went on: 'I agreed. But I wasn't thinking of David and Cindy in that moment. I was thinking about you, Natasha, and Franco . . . and that your husband, Victor, had forgiven you for an affair that was now over. Yesterday, I realised I'd been right all along. There *was* something between you and Franco,' Pearl looked at him now, 'a man who really had loved his wife.'

Franco met Pearl's gaze as she went on.

'But it wasn't an affair between you, was it? It was the shared experience of having forgiven your own spouses, Victor and Caroline, for a relationship that was *meant* to be over . . . but *wasn't*.'

Natasha blinked as if she was waking from a deep sleep. She turned slowly to her husband as she echoed: *'Wasn't?'*

'This is ridiculous,' snapped Victor.

'Is it?' asked Natasha, unsure. 'You told me it was finished between you and Caroline. Long ago. You swore to me?' On Victor's silence, she turned to Franco for an answer. He shook his head. Natasha whispered to him: 'You were trying to tell me what you suspected all along? That morning after Caro hadn't come home? You tried to tell me then, Franco, but I wouldn't listen.'

'I know,' said Franco, gently. 'It was meant to be all over, but after the argument with Caro, I knew she still had feelings for him, but I didn't know for sure and I didn't think for one moment . . .' He was staring coldly at Victor. 'You *killed* her?'

Victor got to his feet. 'Of course I didn't! I just told you, this whole thing is preposterous. One woman's fantasy.' He looked from Pearl to his wife. 'I *couldn't* have done it. I was at home with you, Tash. *Tell* them.'

Natasha gazed up at her husband, towering above her, and remained silent. Victor tried again, this time gently and persuasively: *'Tell* them,' he repeated.

But Natasha shook her head and frowned. 'You got a call,' she began. 'You went out.' She fell silent, then seemed to find the courage to go on. 'You told me it was the gallery, that you wouldn't be gone for long.'

Victor broke in: 'No. No, that's not true!' He stopped, then began again, this time speaking slowly and precisely. 'You told the police the truth that you were with me for the *whole* evening, remember?'

Natasha stared at him, then looked away in shame as she admitted to Pearl: 'I lied.'

'Tash—'

Natasha spoke over her husband, defying him, as she went on, plaintively now. 'You told me it would be easier for us if I told the police you were at home and nothing else. You said it would avoid complications, bad press . . . And I *believed* you.'

She looked searchingly at him now. Pearl did the same as she took up the thread. 'You went to the allotment, Victor. To meet Caroline. Did she tell you about the argument with Franco? That things weren't working out? That she wanted you to confess to Natasha – to tell her you were in love with her?'

Victor looked between Pearl and Natasha – then gave a sudden and incongruous smile. 'I was never in love with Caroline.' He gave a long exhalation and glanced away, then at Natasha. 'And I wish it had never begun but it was always impossible to say no to her. She wouldn't let go, Tash, even after it had ended and she and Franco had moved here. She found ways of bringing me here too . . . rekindling things.'

Natasha forced her eyes tight shut, but Victor continued: 'I *tried* to end it, Tash. I just wanted things to go back to how they were *before* Caro, but she kept making demands, keeping me hooked. She said she always got what she wanted. She gave me a phone to use – unregistered, a burner. She called me on it and said she needed to talk to me so I went to see her at the allotment. She said she knew it was all over between her and Franco, that there was nothing standing in our way any more now that the business was sold. But there was.' Natasha opened her eyes. Victor went on: 'There was you. I love you, Tash. I always have.'

Natasha was staring at him as though he was a stranger. 'You *killed* Caro.'

Victor appeared to struggle with this. 'I didn't mean to . . . but she kept on and on. She said she loved me . . . I couldn't make her listen. She was threatening to tell you *and* Franco. I couldn't let her do that. I had to stop her so I just grabbed hold of the nearest thing and pushed her. She fell backwards, bleeding.' He covered his eyes for a moment. 'I didn't know what to do. I turned and left.'

Franco stared at him. '*Left* her to die.'

'And I found her,' said Ted. 'She was dead when I got there.'

Silence fell. All eyes turned to Victor, who finally admitted: 'She always used that studio on the allotment as a place for us to meet. She said it was one reason it was so special to her.'

Another voice spoke. 'And I saw you both there,' said Florence, getting to her feet.

Joe turned to her, staggered by her admission. 'Flo?'

'I should've spoken up before,' she continued, summoning the courage to go on. 'It was one afternoon when I was down at the allotment. I saw them together as I passed the studio.' She turned to Pearl. 'I wanted to tell you this earlier.' She fought with something inside herself then looked at Joe beside her. 'But I didn't want things to go wrong for you, Joe. Mr Bessant was helping you at the gallery and your pieces were selling.'

'All part of your plan, Victor?' said Pearl. 'Keeping Florence quiet? You knew how much Joe needed those sales.'

Victor Bessant remained silent, then raked his hand through his hair and took a deep breath. 'I knew she'd seen me with Caroline. I was worried about it but Caro was just amused. She was convinced nothing would be said, but . . .'

Pearl realised something. 'Later on you needed to be sure,' she said. 'So your comment to us in the gallery, about supporting members of our local artist community, was as much for Florence's benefit as Joe's?'

Victor turned away but Florence nodded.

'You never told me, Flo . . .' said Joe.

'*Or* me,' said Pearl. 'But remember what Victor had said when we were getting ready to leave the gallery? "*That's the way the world goes round,*" he said, "*helping one another . . .*"' She paused. 'That was surely a veiled reminder to you, Flo, wasn't it? That if you kept quiet about having seen Victor with Caroline, he would continue to help sell Joe's work?'

'I knew what he meant,' said Florence.

'But your conscience must've nagged you and you called me?'

Florence tried to explain. 'Keeping quiet about an affair was one thing, but if I'd thought this had anything at all to do with murder . . . I really *wanted* to tell you, Pearl, but the police arrived and took you away for questioning and I was scared—'

'You should've told me,' Joe insisted.

'I know,' Florence said guiltily. 'I'm telling you now.'

Joe put his arm around her and pulled her close, allowing a moment's distraction, of which Franco took full advantage. Springing to his feet, he raised his arm high above his head, about to bring it down on Victor but Russ Parker was quicker, grabbing Franco's wrist and wrenching a sharp table knife from his hand. 'No!' he ordered. 'Let him rot in prison.'

As the two men looked at Victor, Pearl saw the killer's eyes dart quickly towards the locked door of the restaurant before he glanced around in desperation and took off to escape into the kitchen. The door swung on its hinges after him as Dolly looked at Pearl.

'Back door?'

'Unlocked,' said Pearl, before she took off in pursuit of Bessant as Dolly yelled after her, 'Let the police deal with it!'

Ignoring her mother, Pearl arrived in the kitchen just in time to see Bessant yank open the back door. 'It's no use!' she cried out to him.

Bessant stared back at her then disappeared out the door to escape down the alley outside. Running after him, Pearl suddenly halted in her tracks as she saw a figure appearing at the foot of the alley to block Victor Bessant's path. McGuire grabbed hold of him, spinning Bessant around so that he was facing Pearl as his arms were wrenched behind his back. McGuire met Pearl's gaze as he began to recite the words he knew so well – informing a killer of his rights.

CHAPTER TWENTY-SEVEN

A few days later, Pearl was at the allotment, a pannier resting on her arm. She had gathered some flowers, including sweet peas she had cut from her bamboo wigwam trellis. Glancing over her shoulder, she observed McGuire's progress as he secured a hammock strung between a fence and Dolly's mural on the side of the Nolan cabin. She saw he had managed to get his blond hair cut and had even caught the sun.

'You told me you were going to get Hale to the restaurant to arrest Victor,' she said.

'I know,' McGuire replied, 'but I had to do it myself in case he made a mess of it.'

'And if Bessant had got away?'

'That wouldn't have happened,' McGuire said. 'And for the record, Hale's back to being a DS.'

'And *you*'re back in the driving seat.'

McGuire smiled and shrugged while Pearl studied the new pair of blue jeans he was wearing. 'That leg of yours spent six weeks in plaster and you could have torn the tendon all over again.'

'But I didn't,' said McGuire. 'Though my physio said the same,' he conceded. He sat carefully in the hammock, testing its strength before he swung both legs up into it and lay down. 'She's given me exercises to do,' he went on, 'to build up the muscle.' He slipped on some Ray-Ban sunglasses and settled back in the hammock with his arms behind his head.

Pearl couldn't help smiling. 'Well, you won't do it like that,' she said. 'You'll need some good beach walks. Maybe some sea swimming . . . paddleboarding? But *no* squash.'

Suitably chastened, McGuire swung his legs back so that he was now sitting, not lying, in the hammock. 'No squash,' he agreed.

Propping his sunglasses on his head, he met Pearl's gaze.

'And I'm guessing Hale probably wants to murder you – for making the arrest?' she said.

'I'm sure,' said McGuire, unruffled. 'But Victor Bessant made a full confession once his solicitor arrived at the station. Too much stacked against him – especially after what Florence Brightling had to say. So . . .'

'Case closed?' asked Pearl.

McGuire nodded. 'Until his trial.' He stepped down from the hammock. 'Have you heard from Franco?'

'He's been checking up on Natasha.'

McGuire seemed troubled. 'They should both have owned up about the affair between Caroline and Bessant.'

'You're right,' Pearl agreed. 'But Natasha was in denial and wanted to believe it was all over, and though Franco suspected Caroline still had feelings for Victor, he never once thought he could've killed her.' She added: 'He'd become so used to avoiding bad publicity he wouldn't have wanted news of the affair leaking to the press if there was no real need for it.' She paused and smiled. 'And he insisted on paying me. But I donated his fee to the carnival. It's taking place in a week's time. Would you like to watch it with us at the restaurant? I'm putting on a special menu.'

'Oysters?' asked McGuire, warily.

'Of course!' Pearl said brightly. 'But not compulsory for you.' She added, 'Michael and Vanessa are coming.'

'Joe and Florence?'

Pearl shook her head. 'Joe's working. He's been offered another exhibition – in London this time. All down to Natasha. She seems to be acting for him now as an unofficial agent. He's there with Florence. It's probably the best thing for all of them right now.'

'How about—'

'Cindy and Russ?' said Pearl. 'Something tells me they'll be keeping a low profile for a while. Meanwhile David said he'll be spending the day at the allotment. He's finally going to make a start of clearing his plot. He's looking forward to a new crop – and a new future. And Councillor Radcliffe has managed to get all the complaints dismissed.'

McGuire looked suitably impressed. 'Ratty came up trumps?'

'I'm as surprised as you. It's just a shame he didn't offer to do that right at the start.' She smiled, then suddenly became serious. 'It was good that the CPS decided not to prosecute Ted. He's moved in with Madge to take care of her and make sure she takes her meds. He said it's only temporary, but something tells me they may be together for far longer. Some things are meant to be.' She turned to face McGuire.

'Yes,' he said, his tone shifting to something more serious. 'She might think he's just there to take care of her . . . but it's much more than that.'

'Is it?' asked Pearl, catching the look in his eye.

'They're like two sides of the same coin.'

'Yin and yang?'

'Light and shade.'

Pearl moved closer to him. 'He's a good man, protecting her, doing everything he did to save her.'

'But he had it all wrong – because she didn't need saving after all.'

'Not in the way he thought,' said Pearl. 'But she needs him. More than ever.'

'Does she?' asked McGuire.

The question hung between them until Pearl nodded. McGuire leaned in to kiss her, and when they broke apart, he continued to remain lost in her beautiful moonstone-grey eyes.

Pearl spoke softly: 'When we were talking about Franco and Natasha, you said I should know the signs, when there's something between two people.'

McGuire arched an eyebrow. 'And?'

Pearl set down her pannier. 'When Franco made his TV appeal with Hale on the news, and described what Caroline had meant to him, I knew he was speaking the truth, but there was still so much confusion with everything else. Later, when I was sitting with you at the harbour, I tried my hardest to see through all that – and suddenly everything seemed clear because the clues were all there, as they'd been all along. Love and money . . . Russ and Cindy . . . Ted's mobility scooter . . . and I *knew* Franco couldn't have killed his wife *or* been unfaithful with Natasha because he loved Caroline too much. I'd just been looking at things the wrong way round. Caroline had been the one having the affair – with Victor. She didn't want it to end – and she was used to getting what she wanted. But not this time.'

McGuire observed Pearl, aware of her satisfaction at having solved yet another mystery. For a few moments, he seemed lost for words until he placed his hands on her shoulders. His eyes scanned hers. 'Pearl, this is difficult.'

'What is?' she asked, unnerved.

'I know I asked you to marry me,' he said, 'but I've had a chance to do some thinking and I really don't want to take over your life. If you're happier staying single, living in that cottage of yours . . . doing what you enjoy doing—'

Pearl laid a finger gently on his lips. 'Why don't we see how things work out?'

'Is that what you want?'

'You said yourself we've always been the victims of bad timing.'

'And now?'

'Now . . .' Pearl braced herself before she went on '. . . it's time for change,' she said, with confidence. 'I really think we could move forward, don't you?' She smiled. 'After all, you said there'd be no walking down any aisle until that cast was off . . . and Mum's still after buying a nice hat.'

McGuire's eyes took on a sudden sparkle. 'I reckon she'd look good in one.' He returned Pearl's smile, then asked: 'And what about Charlie?'

'I heard from him this morning,' said Pearl. 'He's coming back tomorrow. Things haven't worked out with the new girlfriend, Cerys, but he's still had a good time. He'll be needing his old room at home – but only until he gets himself sorted.'

McGuire took this in. 'So . . .' he began, his hands moving from Pearl's shoulders to her bare arms '. . . we're really going to do this?'

Pearl nodded. 'And I think we should do it properly. In church. St Alfred's in the high street. We'll have a big reception. Good food . . . the best!' she added, enthused by the thought. 'Some entertainment. And I was thinking it should be a spring wedding.'

'Spring?'

'Just as the flowers are coming into blossom.' She reached into her pannier and took out a white rose, breathing in its sweet scent, then allowing McGuire to do the same.

He locked eyes with her. 'Spring,' he repeated. 'So, we have a lot of planning to do before then.'

'You bet,' said Pearl. 'And *you* have a lot of training to do too – *if* you're going to walk down that aisle without falling over.'

McGuire gave a slow smile. 'Whatever happens, I reckon I can count on you to prop me up.'

'Don't worry,' said Pearl, moving closer to him, feeling his arms tightening around her body now. 'That's a given.'

ACKNOWLEDGEMENTS

For this, the tenth novel in the Whitstable Pearl Mystery series, I find myself grateful to many people.

First, I'd like to thank my friend and fellow crime writer, Glen Laker, who has penned episodes of *Vera*, starring Brenda Blethyn, as well as co-writing *The Chelsea Detective*, a crime series made for Acorn TV, the same streaming service that makes *Whitstable Pearl* – the TV series based on my books. As coincidences go, Glen also lives in Whitstable and happens to have an allotment plot. Once I had explained to him that I was about to write *Murder at the Allotment*, he very kindly offered me an enlightening and enjoyable grand tour of the site. Glen has also previously partnered me in an event at Whitstable's very own literary festival, WhitLit, which I'm pleased to report has now returned after a four-year hiatus. I'm extremely grateful to WhitLit's founder and director, Victoria Falconer, for having invited me to become a patron of the festival, with celebrity journalist

Richard Barber, to whom I am also grateful not only for interviewing me for a WhitLit event but also for writing a wonderful double-page spread for the *Daily Mail*'s Weekend magazine about *Whitstable Pearl*, the TV series.

The first season of *Whitstable Pearl* began streaming in May 2021, starring Kerry Godliman as Pearl, Howard Charles as McGuire and Frances Barber as Dolly. I'm very thankful to the team at Buccaneer Media, which includes Tony Wood and Richard Tulk-Hart, who produce the series for Acorn TV and who kindly gave me a role in the production as executive producer. Since then, there has been a second season, which has been performing well all over the world, so I give huge thanks to all the cast and crew members for bringing my characters to the small screen in such a gripping and entertaining series. I am also thrilled to report that at the time of writing a third season of *Whitstable Pearl* has just been green-lit.

Warm thanks also go to two Kent-based novelists: fellow crime writer and real-life detective Lisa Cutts, and author and screenwriter Mark Stay, for teaming up with me for some very enjoyable author events.

Thanks also to festival directors Denise Martin-Harker, Jaye Nolan and Jodi Eeles for inviting me to take part in author events at the Broadstairs Book Festival, Murderous Medway and Maidstone Literary Festival, respectively.

A big thank-you always goes to Clare Connerton and all her hardworking staff at the independent book shop Harbour Books in Whitstable, including Graeme Bosley and Katey 'Kapers' Pugh, as well as to Jacqui Delbaere at the Little Green Book Shop in Herne Bay.

Many thanks also to Whitstable wood sculptor Nigel Hobbins, for inspiring me regarding Joe Fuller's work in this book – and also to Ian Venables, who, after hearing news about this book, invited me to meet everyone at Westgate-on-Sea allotments and give out prizes for tallest sunflower and biggest pumpkin!

I remain ever grateful to Dominic King of BBC Radio Kent for his friendship and support for my books and the TV series, which includes a special feature that examined my use of music in the Whitstable Pearl Mysteries with a fantastic interview with Daniel Leeson Harding, the Director of Music Performance at Kent University, and musical contributions from the wonderfully talented mezzo soprano, Michelle Harris.

My gratitude goes, as ever, to my publishing director and editor, Krystyna Green, at Little, Brown Book Group for having faith in these novels in the first instance, and to my agent, Michelle Kass, who has been a rock for me throughout the last thirty years, with her dedicated associates, Russell Franklin, Tishna Molla and Melissa Nock, not forgetting my husband, Kas Kasparian, for all his proofreading duties.

Finally, my sincere thanks and appreciation go to all those who enjoy my Whitstable Pearl Mystery novels – because an author is nothing without readers.

AUTHOR'S NOTE

While I have used as a setting for this book an allotment site off Joy Lane in Whitstable, close to Prospect Field, I have taken author's licence in doing so, having given Pearl and Dolly a plot there back in Book 2 of the series – *Murder-on-Sea*.

The real allotments in this area of Whitstable are on much larger areas of land and consist of many more plots and holders than I have cited with my suspects.

Whitstable has at least three areas of allotments, always a joy to behold when I pass them, particularly in the summer months when they are full of blossom and produce.

We are also very lucky to enjoy an area of land known as Stream Walk Community Garden, the ethos of which is biodiversity and sustainability. Managed by members of our local community, the garden is chemical-free and produces all variety of vegetables, salad ingredients and flowers, which can be bought by the public on Thursday mornings.

Duncan Down at the top of Borstal Hill in Whitstable is a thirteen-acre area of protected land, designated as Village Green and managed by local volunteers. It also features in Book 6 of the series, *Murder on the Downs*.

While it's true that so much of our green space is vanishing in the face of an increasing number of property developments, Whitstable still has several important wildlife corridors, including on our castle grounds, across the golf course and along the railway embankment mentioned in this book. It was on the latter that we, as a community in Whitstable, successfully fought the clearance of trees and vegetation by Network Rail during the bird breeding season of 2012. The embankment lies at the foot of my own home, a haven for all manner of wildlife, including the stag beetle, a globally endangered species, and in the early hours of 12 May that year, I and two friends chained ourselves to an oak tree to prevent chainsaws felling the embankment trees, with the stag beetles hatching – as if on cue. After saving the trees that day, supported in our protest by hundreds of people in our town, thousands of starlings then gathered in nightly murmurations in the area, in a way that led many Whitstable residents to believe they were giving thanks.

No one quite knows why starlings perform these breathtaking displays, swooping and swerving in the sky in fascinating patterns, but of one thing I am sure:

we too can gather and achieve beautiful and seemingly impossible results if we flock together to protect our wildlife and our precious environment.